GW00672043

The Road to Solace

SAMANTHA COLE

Author's Note

The Road to Solace was formerly titled *The Friar*.

Acknowledgements

My beta readers:
Allena, Brandie, Charla, Debbie, Felisha, Jen, Jessica,
Joanne, Julie, Katie, Kelle, and Milynn.
Love every one of you!

My editor, Eve—*Hugs*

Lucky 13 Book Reviews and News—for stepping in and
helping at the last minute!

My PA, Maria—love ya! Thanks for putting up with me!

My Sexy Six-Pack Sirens Facebook group for their shout
outs, whip cracking, and everyday fun. I love each one of
you from the bottom of my heart!

And as always, last, but far from least, my readers. Without
you, I would have never have come this far. I hope you
enjoy Adam and Sage's story as much as I loved writing it.

Chapter One

"Forgive me, Father, for I have sinned. Please ... please, help me."

Kneeling at the altar of the small chapel, he stared up at the huge wooden crucifix and prayed everything had been a nightmare—a horrible, reversible nightmare. Holy water dripped from his hands and trailed back to the baptismal font where he'd been trying to cleanse the invisible blood from his skin for the past four hours. However, it was useless—his flesh and his soul were stained and would be forever more.

The silence in the centuries-old stone church was louder than anything he'd ever experienced. It permeated his thoughts. He was drowning in wave after wave of remorse and despair. Of evil and horror.

They were coming for him. Why it hadn't happened yet, he wasn't sure—but they would come looking for him soon. Seconds had given way to minutes in his mind. Minutes had become hours.

Why, Father? Why was I there? Why didn't you stop him? Why didn't you stop me?

His heavy head hung low as he clasped his hands together, extending toward the bronze figure suspended on the wooden cross by metal stakes driven into the hands and feet. His knees ached from the cold, hard floor, but he refused to stand. He deserved the pain and so much more for what he'd done.

At thirty-four, almost his entire adult life had been dedicated to serving the Lord. His faith was the one thing in which he'd found comfort, but today that faith had been tested, and he'd failed miserably. The devil inside him had taken over his mind, body, and, yes, his soul. It didn't matter that the evil had been in response to an even greater evil. One which had no remorse. One which had harmed an innocent child.

Burning tears blurred his vision and rolled down his cheeks before falling to the floor to mix with the small puddles on the granite tile. "I'm sorry, Father. Please help me. Tell me what I must do."

His life as he'd known it was over. Part of him wanted to run and hide, but that went against his morals . . . his code of ethics. Despite everything that had happened earlier in the day, he still had them and would abide by them. He would take whatever punishment and penance he faced— with the courts and with the Holy Father. And maybe someday he would receive His forgiveness.

The scraping and clanking of the large wood and iron doors at the rear of the church told him his time was up. They had finally come for him. He fought the urge to flee. Multiple footsteps approached as, out of the corner of his eye to his left, he saw a uniformed officer emerge from the sacristy. The side door to his right, leading to the parking lot, opened, and another officer filled the entryway. They were covering every exit. Didn't they know he would go willingly? That he wouldn't fight what he deserved?

The purposeful footsteps stopped several feet behind him, and he waited, holding on to his last moments of freedom.

"Adam."

He winced at the sound of his name spoken so softly. He should have known Shane Stewart would come for him. The man was the only person left in the world whom he considered to be family. While they weren't blood-related, they'd spent their formative teenage years in the same foster home and remained close as their lives had led them in different directions. And now, they were on opposite sides of the law.

Adam touched his fingers to his forehead, heart, left shoulder, and then the right. Praying for strength and guidance, he slowly stood and turned around. His best friend was accompanied by another plainclothes detective and two uniformed officers—six men in total had come for him. He ignored the others as his gaze met Shane's. The pain, regret, and sadness he saw there were almost unbearable. "I'm sorry, my friend."

When Shane didn't say or do anything, his partner stepped forward and pulled a pair of shiny, metal handcuffs from his sports jacket. As the man rounded behind him, Adam placed his hands at his lower back, his brown eyes never leaving his friend's sad, green ones.

The detective fastened the cuffs around his bare wrists with resounding clicks which echoed throughout the chapel. "Brother Adam Westfield. You are under arrest for the murder of Brother Andre Santiago. You have the right to remain silent . . ."

———— ♥ ————

Five Years and Four Months Later . . .

"So, do you have plans on where you'll go from here, Brother Adam?" Jose Ferrara finished gathering the prayer books left behind by the other prisoners who came to the morning's spiritual service. The numbers usually varied, but today had been a full house as they'd come to say goodbye to the man who had given them guidance and understanding these past few years.

Today was Adam's release day. A day he'd been looking forward to and dreading for months now. He'd served a little over half his sentence. With time off for good behavior and overcrowding in the prison system, the parole board had approved his early release. In less than two hours, he'd be a free man. A shudder passed through him, and he shook off the combined feelings of anticipation and anxiety.

Taking the bound missals from the convicted car thief, Adam stacked them on the closet shelf and shut the door. "Not really. Think I'm just going to travel a bit. Enjoy the things I've missed in here."

"Like what? I mean, I know what I've missed, but everyone has their own list."

He exited the prison library, heading back to Cell Block C with Jose on his heels. They were buzzed through several heavy, locked doors, and some of the guards wished him good luck along the way. He'd been a model prisoner during his time there and had earned the respect of the guards as well as the inmates.

4

When he had first arrived at Sing-Sing Correctional Facility in Ossining, NY, several things had prevented him from being a target for the thugs who loved to assault and/or rape newcomers as a sick version of a welcoming committee. One—word had quickly spread that he was a Franciscan Brother, and some drew the line at assaulting a man of God. Two—the man he'd killed was a child molester, the scum of the earth according to most inmates, therefore making Adam some sort of hero in their mindset. Three —the one man who had tried to take him on a few days after his arrival had learned the hard way that Adam held a black belt in Krav Maga, the martial arts which had originated in Israeli Defense Forces.

From the time they were fourteen until adulthood, Adam and Shane's foster father had been a police officer. Harry Brooks had enrolled them in the classes to give them an outlet for their teenage energy and angst and to instill the discipline that both had lacked up to that point. He'd even taught them boxing, wrestling, and how to defend themselves against dirty street fighting. The training had kept them out of the trouble most kids their age had been getting into and ultimately pointed them in the direction their lives would lead. Although, Harry would probably be rolling over in his grave if he knew where Adam had ended up.

"Things like the sunrise and sunset over the ocean or a mountain. The smell of fresh-cut grass. A child's laughter." He let out a small chuckle. "A poached egg."

"Ha! I'd take any egg that wasn't powdered. But fuck that, man. I just want to see my woman again and be able to fu . . . well, you know, any time I want."

The corner of Adam's mouth ticked upward. Jose always seemed to remember he was talking to a former

5

man of the cloth a second too late. But he managed to catch himself more often than not. "I get the gist, yeah."

"What about you? I mean, you weren't always a brother, right? Before all that, did you ever have a girlfriend?"

While his vow of celibacy had been a part of him since he'd realized his role in life was to be spent in the Brotherhood, he did have a few experiences with the opposite sex during his teens. "Kelly Adams. We met and dated in high school. Everyone teased us, saying if we got married, I would be Mr. Adam Adams."

Jose laughed. "That's funny. Was she hot?"

"I believe the phrase you would use is 'she was smoking.'"

They entered Cell Block C's indoor rec area. The cells were located around the perimeter of three floors. The higher two levels overlooked the large open room where men of all ages, races, and sizes found something to do to whittle away the endless days. Some were watching the few TV channels they were allowed. Others read, played cards or chess, and worked out on the weight benches. It was pouring rain for the third straight day. Otherwise, most of them would be out in the courtyard on the first day of spring. A few had ventured out briefly just for a change of scenery.

"Where's she now?"

Adam shrugged. "Last I heard, she's living in Florida, happily married with a few kids."

Jose was about to ask another question but was interrupted when one, then two, then more of the inmates started clapping. Soon the entire block thundered with applause. Adam knew it was their way of celebrating his release. It wasn't done for everyone, just men who'd gained the ultimate respect of their peers. His cellmate, Justin Bauman, stepped forward and handed him a crudely wrapped gift as the others cheered.

"Bro-ther Ad-am!" *Clap. Clap. Clap, clap, clap.* "Bro-ther Ad-am!" *Clap. Clap. Clap, clap, clap.*

While he'd officially resigned from the Brotherhood in disgrace after his conviction, most of the inmates had chosen to keep using the title—especially those who'd embraced their faith in the Lord.

Embarrassed at the impromptu party, complete with a hastily made cake from the prison's kitchen, Adam waved and tried to quiet the crowd down. "Thank you. Thanks."

It was a full minute before the shouts changed. "Speech! Speech!"

He grinned. "If you would all shut up, I can give you one!"

Laughter faded to silence as he stared at the present in his hands. Leaving it wrapped for a moment, he swallowed and searched for the right words. "These past few years have been a form of hell, as most of you can attest to. But somewhere along the line, I've found friendships I never expected. I thank you for that. Now that I'm leaving, someone will have to step up to the plate as chess king around here." A few chuckles scattered throughout the cell block. "Whether you're here as a lifer or someone who will one day be released from this hole, please do your best to become someone you can be proud of. Someone God can be proud of. Work hard. Respect others. And may God bless you and keep you safe."

His words were met with another round of applause. While he knew many would turn a deaf ear to his advice, others would try to heed it. If only one person found comfort in his words, then they were worth saying. Tearing open the package, he was stunned to find a leather-bound copy of one of his favorite books—*Death Be Not Proud*. He'd read his foster father's copy many times while living with Harry. However, after the man's line-of-duty death, the book was accidentally donated with the rest of his extensive collection to several nursing homes and veteran hospitals. Adam had found a copy in the prison library and reread it every few months.

A lump developed in his throat, and he coughed to clear it. "Um . . . wow. I didn't expect this . . . and I'm not sure I want to know where it came from . . . but thanks. Every time I read it, I'll think of all of you."

A little over an hour later, his meager possessions were packed into two shopping bags, and he signed a receipt for the items which had been stored in the property office. He was escorted out to the yard—the rain had temporarily subsided, but a mist still hung in the air—and up to the main gates, where several more guards wished him well. The last huge blockade opened, and he took the final few steps leading to his freedom. As he was pulled into his best friend's embrace, the metal gate clanged closed behind him.

Standing an inch shorter than Adam's six-foot-three, Shane slapped him on the back several times before releasing him again. "It's damn good to see you on this side of the fence again. How does it feel?"

"Honestly . . . weird."

"Ha! Yeah, well, you'll get used to it. C'mon. Let's get out of here. I'm taking you for lunch, complete with steak, potatoes, and beer."

Chapter Two

D*amn, it's hot.*

Sage Hammond wiped the sweat from her brow before pitching more hay into one of the horses' stalls. Two weeks before the first day of summer, the heat in Oklahoma was spiking above average for this time of the year. It was just past 7:00 a.m., and she was already wishing she'd worn a tank top instead of one of Mark's large T-shirts. While she'd given away most of her husband's clothes after his death two and a half years ago, she'd kept some of his funny shirts to wear when she was missing him. Today's navy blue shirt proclaimed, "Lead Me Not Into Temptation . . . Oh Hell, Follow Me, I Know A Shortcut." It'd been one of his favorites.

Behind her, the ranch's prize sire nickered impatiently for Sage to let him out of his stall and lead him to the pasture. Last night's wind and torrential rain had forced her ranch foreman to bring the horses in for safekeeping. Unfortunately, it had done nothing to cool the high temperatures. "I'm coming, Gino. You know your pregnant girlfriend has to get some fresh hay and feed first." The horse nickered again, obviously not impressed he had to wait a few more seconds so Sage could finish caring for Diamond Lil.

The one-hundred-fifty-acre Heaven's Pastures was an Appaloosa breeding ranch and currently home to eleven mares, four of which were ready to foal within the next two weeks, and two stallions. In addition to the breeding stock, two older quarter horses were used for riding around the ranch. The other animals on the property consisted of a dozen sheep, six llamas, eight chickens, one rooster, two barn cats, and one very active border collie who kept them all in line.

The land had been in her husband's family for seven generations as a small cattle ranch until his great-grandfather switched it over to horse breeding. Five years ago, Mark and Sage had added the llamas, which were sheared for their wool, similar to the sheep. There was a good market for the fibrous coats, and the income helped offset the sale of the yearling horses, which was normally at the end of the summer each year. Mark's great-grandmother had dubbed the ranch Heaven's Pastures because of the family's cemetery at the north end of the property. Sage's son and daughter would hopefully one day continue with the family business—if she managed to hold onto it for that long.

After finishing with the horses' feed and water, Sage fed the rest of the animals and then collected the eggs from the chicken coop. Her cook and housekeeper, Maddie, would need them for her baking tomorrow. The next day was Sunday, and their church was having a bake sale to help raise money for the choir to attend a state-wide competition in July. Maddie Tanner and her husband, Evan, had worked for the Hammond family since Mark had been a boy. Childless, they'd lived in a small cottage on the property for close to thirty years, and Sage didn't know what she would have done without the couple since Mark's death.

Striding to the rear entrance to her two-story house, she heard Benji, their dog, barking out front. As she climbed the steps to the porch, the door swung open and eight-year-old Matthew announced, "Mom, someone is walking up the driveway."

That was odd. The ranch was six miles from town, and her nearest neighbors were two miles away. No one just walked to their place. She handed her son the basket of eggs. "Take these to Maddie, then go wash up for breakfast, and I'll see who it is."

The screen door slammed closed behind her as she walked through the house to the front door. Sure enough, a man was coming up the long, dirt driveway, carrying a military duffel bag over his shoulder. She didn't recognize him, but he appeared to be in his late thirties. Dressed in worn jeans, hiking boots, and a gray T-shirt, he was about six-foot-three and physically fit. A baseball cap covered his hair and shaded his face.

While there was nothing about his posture that made her uneasy, just the fact he was a stranger had her hurrying into her bedroom. She retrieved Mark's Smith & Wesson 9mm and its belt holster from the safe in her closet and clipped it to her jeans at the small of her back before returning to the front door. Swinging it open, she proceeded out to the top of the steps and waited for the man to approach. Benji was still barking as he joined her on the porch.

When the man got within twenty feet of the house, the dog ran down the steps, and his bark turned into a growl. Sage stiffened, but the man stopped dead in his tracks. He stood perfectly still as the dog took a few cautious steps forward, sniffing the air. "Hey, boy. Come check me out. I'm not here to hurt you or your family."

He squatted down and let the protective dog sniff his hand. Sage's shoulders relaxed a little when Benji's tail began wagging furiously, and he licked the stranger's hand. The dog had always been a great judge of character.

When the dog rolled over onto his back, the man scratched the proffered stomach, then lifted his gaze to Sage. "Hi. Sorry for the unannounced visit. I'm looking for Sage Hammond."

Crossing her arms, she stared into his soft brown eyes. There was nothing but kindness in them—well, maybe a little bit of sadness and loneliness. She recognized it because that's what she saw reflecting in her mirror most mornings. "I'm Sage Hammond. Who are you, and how do you know my name?"

Standing again, he removed his cap, wiped the sweat on his brow with his forearm, and then set the cap back atop his dark-blond head. "My name is Adam Westfield. I spoke with Reverend Stevens this morning, and he said you were looking for someone to help out around the ranch. I'd like to apply for the job if it's still available."

It was true. She was in desperate need of help on the ranch. The last two men she'd hired had both up and left without any notice. One after two weeks, the other after only a few days. She knew ranching was hard work and not for everyone, but the least they could have done was tell her why they'd left. "You're not from around here, are you?"

He chuckled. "No, ma'am, I'm not. My New York accent gives me away every time, doesn't it?"

Her mouth tilted up in a small smile. "It was pretty much my first clue."

"Well, please don't hold it against me. I'm a hard worker and a fast learner."

"Is that so?" Even though Benji had approved of him, she still didn't know the man. But Lord, she hoped he was the answer to her prayers. There was so much work that needed to be done, and the heavier stuff was getting too much for Evan and her. "Tell me more about yourself, Mr. Westfield. Why is a New York drifter in our little town of Rosewood, Oklahoma, looking for a job that pays very little besides room and board?"

He shrugged and grinned, two dimples appearing on his tanned cheeks. "Why not? Everyone's got to work somewhere, right?" When she didn't respond, he dropped his duffel at his feet and held his hands out to the side. His smile faded. "Okay. Here's the deal. I was released from prison several months ago, and I'm looking for a way to start my life over again."

"Prison?" Her shoulders tensed again at his confession as a shiver of fear coursed through her. She hoped she wasn't going to have to pull out her gun. While she wasn't thrilled he'd been incarcerated, she did give him kudos for putting it out in front instead of hiding it from her. She didn't know many people who would admit that to someone they just met, especially when they were looking for a job. "Why were you in prison?"

"Prison? That's so cool!"

Sage swung around to see her son had been watching and listening from inside the screen door. "Matthew! Go back to the kitchen!"

"Aww, Moooom."

"Now!"

Pouting, he spun on his heel and stomped his way through the house. Sage turned back to face the stranger, who hadn't moved. She shook her head. "I'm sorry, Mr. Westfield, but an ex-con is not someone I want around my children. I'm sorry you made the trip out here for nothing."

A look of compassion came across his handsome face. "No worries, ma'am. I understand completely." He tilted his head toward the old well in her front yard. "Do you mind if I take a drink before I head out?"

It was the least she could do. It *was* a six-mile walk from town unless someone had been nice enough to give him a lift. "No, I don't mind. Just crank up the bucket. The water is fresh."

He tipped the edge of his ball cap. "Thank you. I appreciate it."

Picking up his duffel, he swung it over his shoulder again and ambled over to the stone well with Benji on his heels.

———— ♥ ————

ADAM DROPPED HIS BAG BY THE WELL BEFORE GRABBING THE CRANK handle. Someone had oiled it recently because it turned easily. It wasn't long before the filled bucket reached the top, and he set the brake to keep it there. Removing the bucket from its hook, he set it on the wall of the well. Cupping his hands, he dipped them in the water and then brought them to his lips. The cool water felt wonderful in his parched mouth and throat. After drinking his fill, he used more of the water to rinse his face. While Reverend Stevens had been nice enough to let him use the shower at the rectory, the walk from town in the heat and humidity had left him sweaty and grimy again.

After replacing the bucket and sending it back to the bottom of the well, he grabbed his foster father's old army duffel and hefted it onto his shoulder. Reverend Stevens had suggested there might be another rancher not far from here willing to take him on for some menial work. Adam had been hitchhiking across the states for the last three months, taking temporary jobs wherever he found them. Then after collecting his pay, whether it'd been for a few hours or days, he would move on. Several of the people he'd worked for had begged him to stay on—he hadn't lied about being a hard worker and fast learner—but something inside him had urged him to leave each time. He didn't know where he was headed, but he felt something more was waiting for him somewhere. Until he found it, he would continue roaming the highways and back country roads.

Glancing over his shoulder, he saw Ms. Hammond waiting for him to leave. Her five-foot-six frame stood rigid as her long, medium-brown hair lifted in the light wind. She was a beautiful woman, still holding onto the curves from at least one pregnancy. He may have been celibate for years, but he was still a healthy heterosexual male, so it didn't surprise him when his body reacted to her attractiveness. Reverend Stevens had told him the woman was a widowed mother, and there was a couple who also lived on the property while working for her.

He tipped his cap toward her. "Thank you, ma'am. You have a nice day."

"You, too."

"By the way, I like your shirt."

He didn't wait for a reply as she glanced down, probably trying to remember which shirt she was wearing. Hoofing it again, he hadn't gotten more than a hundred feet when the sound of an engine coming up the drive, accompanied by a veil of dust, caught his attention. Ms. Hammond obviously saw it as well, and if her spat out "shit" was any indication, she wasn't happy about it. Stepping to the side of the drive to avoid being run over, he watched as two men in a black Ford pickup drove by. Something niggled in his brain and made him decide to stick around for a few minutes to make sure there was no trouble. Especially when he noticed Ms. Hammond pull a handgun from behind her back. *Oh, hell, this can't be good.*

Tossing his duffel over the fence of the front pasture, he took a few steps back toward the house as the two men climbed out of the truck. Ms. Hammond kept the weapon at her side and pointed to the ground, but Adam felt she wouldn't hesitate to use it if she had to.

"Get the hell off my property, Bart, or you'll be patching up bullet holes in that brand-new truck of yours. And take your attack dog with you."

Oh, yeah. Definitely not good. Since she was glaring at the tall man with the black cowboy hat, who'd been the front seat passenger, Adam assumed he was "Bart." That meant the shorter driver in the brown Stetson was the "attack dog"—whatever she meant by that. Both men were in their forties and dressed in typical ranching clothes—jeans, cowboy boots, and due to the hot temperature, T-shirts.

Bart held his hands out to his sides. "Now, come on, Sage. There's no need for the gun. I'm just here to make you another offer on the ranch. You know you'll have to sell soon if you can't get caught up on the mortgage with the bank."

Her eyes went wide with shocked annoyance. "Who the hell told you that?"

The man shrugged. "You know how the small-town

information mill is. Mark's medical bills had to run over a hundred thousand—anyone with a brain could figure that out. I'm just trying to help you out. I'm more than willing to give you a fair price for the land. You'll be able to settle with the bank and still have a little left over. If the bank forecloses, you'll be left with nothing. Hell, you can't even keep the hired help working for you. Nobody wants to work for the peanuts you're paying."

Adam stopped a few feet behind the arrogant ass and crossed his arms. "Well, almost nobody."

Surprised, Bart pivoted around to face him. Apparently, the man hadn't noticed him or didn't realize he was still there. "Who the hell are you?"

"Adam Westfield. And you are?"

The rancher eyed him curiously from head to toe before answering. "Bart Sherman. I own Rosewood Hills Ranch up the road. You must be new in town."

Behind the man, Ms. Hammond came down to the bottom step and thankfully lowered her weapon. "He is, and he's also my new employee."

The rancher's eyes never left Adam's. "Is that so?"

He wasn't going to say otherwise. Ms. Hammond may have changed her mind about hiring him or was just saying that to get rid of the man. Either way . . . "Yes, sir, it is."

"Harrumph." Sherman put his hands on his hips. "You must be crazy to work for free or just shy of it."

Ignoring the woman's sputter of disbelief at the statement, Adam didn't back down. "Well, some people may question my sanity, but I don't. As for the pay, it's a good thing money isn't on my list of coveted things I need in life. I'll take work wherever I can get it."

"Well, don't plan on keeping this one for long. Either Sage sells to me, or the bank will be foreclosing soon. When that happens, feel free to come over to my ranch. I'm sure we can find some work for you there."

Movement at the side of the house caught his eye, and Adam's gaze shifted to see an older man standing quietly but watching the confrontation with keen interest. A shotgun lay cradled in his arms. The man was probably one half of the couple who worked on the ranch, who Reverend Stevens had told him about. "I'm much obliged. If and when that time comes, I'll think about it." *Not likely.* "Now, if you'll excuse us, we have some work to do."

Sherman didn't seem very happy about being dismissed and turned back to face Ms. Hammond. "You better think real hard about my offer, Sage, before it's too late." With a glance over his shoulder at Adam, the man climbed up into the truck as his driver did the same. The tires kicked up an angry cloud of dirt as the vehicle did a U-turn and headed out to the main road.

Now that the other men were gone, the bravado in Ms. Hammond's face diminished somewhat. Not wanting her to feel obligated to go through with what had been a spur-of-the-moment statement about him being her new employee, Adam walked back to retrieve his duffel. Hoisting it on his shoulder one more time, he followed the fading trail of dust the truck had left in its wake.

"Hey! Wait a minute! Hold up!"

He stopped and turned to see her running up to him. Her handgun was nowhere in sight—she must have holstered it again behind her back. In silence, he waited for her to catch up to him.

Halting a few feet away from him, she took a deep breath and let it out. "I-I'm sorry about that. You didn't have to get involved in my crap, but thank you for doing so."

His shoulders lifted in a shrug. "No worries. I hope everything works out for you."

When he began to leave again, she reached out and touched his upper arm, stopping him in his tracks. "Wait. I mean . . . if you're still interested in the job, I could really use the help. As Bart said, it doesn't pay a lot, but my housekeeper is an excellent cook, and you'd have your own cabin here on the property."

He tilted his head and studied her. While she was still wary of him, he saw something else in her eyes . . . hope. Lowering his duffel again, he stood tall and met her gaze. "I was arrested for killing a man who was in the process of molesting a young boy. It was a man I'd worked beside for many years, and I guess you can say I just snapped. I've regretted it ever since and will continue to do so until my dying day. While I never would've let him get away with what he'd done, I wish I hadn't taken his life. I pled guilty to manslaughter and served a little over five years of a ten-year sentence. Other than that, I've never intentionally broken the law before, and I hope I never have to again. I guess the only other thing I should mention is I go to church every Sunday. I'd appreciate it if I could have that time off from work. If you still want to hire me, that is."

After his first sentence, her mouth had dropped open, but she'd let him continue. He gave her a moment to digest what he'd told her and for her to decide if it was something she could live with. He would understand if she changed her mind once again.

"Um . . . okay. Is there a way I can confirm what you told me? I mean, I do have my family to think about."

"Yes, ma'am. You can call the Middletown Police Department in New York and ask for Detective Shane Stewart—he should be working today. He's not only my foster brother, but he's also the officer who arrested me. He'll answer any questions you have. You can also call the warden at the Sing-Sing Correctional Facility in Ossining, New York. He'll confirm I was a model prisoner during my stay there."

She briefly bit her bottom lip. "What about the internet or newspapers?"

"The boy's father is the head editor of the local newspaper. He made sure the entire incident never appeared in print or on the internet. He had friends in the courts and was able to get the case files sealed. You won't be able to access them without a court order." He paused. "I know this makes you uneasy, so I'll understand if you don't want to hire me."

"No! I mean, yes, I'm a little wary—you're a stranger, after all—but if what you told me is the truth, then I'd be willing to hire you. On a trial basis, of course."

The corners of his mouth ticked upward. "Of course. I can wait here if you want to make those calls, Ms. Hammond."

"Sage, please." She stepped to the side and gestured toward the house with her hand. "And why don't you come up to the porch? I'll bring you out some breakfast while I'm on the phone. It's the least I can do for helping me deal with that jackass, Bart."

With a genuine smile forming on his face, he dipped his head. "Much obliged, ma'am . . . I mean, Sage. Thank you."

Chapter Three

Hanging up the phone in her office, Sage contemplated her conversations with first the prison warden and then Detective Stewart. Both men had stated exactly what Adam had told her—he'd killed a man who'd been molesting a child, confessed to the crime, and pled guilty at a plea bargain hearing instead of making the child testify. He'd been a model prisoner, counseling other inmates during his time there. His sentence had been reduced for good behavior and the unlikelihood of repeating his crime.

While she was sure the men had kept some of the more brutal elements of the incident from her, it was obvious Adam had reacted as most people would if walking into the same situation. Detective Stewart had mentioned that when Adam had pulled the sexual offender off the boy, he'd thrown him across the room. The pervert had gotten back up, and a struggle ensued between the two men. At some point, Adam had punched the other man in the face, causing him to fall and strike his head on a piece of furni-

21

ture—he never got up again. Adam had called 9-1-1 to report the incident and to get help for both the offender and his victim. He then waited in a nearby church for the police to arrest him.

Stewart had said if Adam's case had gone to trial, he probably would have been found not guilty of murder due to the circumstances, but he'd refused to go that route—opting to pay for his crime by pleading to the lesser charge of manslaughter. He also told her Adam was the kindest, most honorable man he knew. The warden had made a similar statement as well—he'd become well acquainted with the prisoner and even played chess with him a time or two.

Making her decision, she stood and returned the 9mm to her bedroom safe before heading out to the porch to talk to him. She wasn't surprised to see Evan Tanner chatting with the newcomer. When she opened the screen door, both men stood at her arrival. Evan gave her a nod and wink before descending the steps and proceeding to the backyard. That had been his way of giving his approval —Adam had clearly made an impression on the man who wasn't easily swayed.

Smiling, Sage eyed Adam's empty plate and an untouched bowl of grits. "Maddie is an excellent cook, isn't she? I take it you're not a fan of grits." The older woman had heaped the plate with bacon, eggs, hash browns, and toast with blueberry jam.

He chuckled. "Um . . . no, I'm not. Haven't been able to acquire a taste for them yet, but everything else was delicious. Please thank her for me."

"You'll be able to do that yourself at dinnertime . . . that is if you still want the job." She rattled off what his duties would entail, the meager pay, and a few other things. "Are you still interested?"

Taking off his cap, he nodded, then ran a hand through his dark-blond hair. It was thick and wavy, and for a split second, she wished it was her hand touching it before he covered it up again.

"Absolutely . . . and thank you. Where would you like me to start?"

Shaking off her wayward thoughts, she gestured to his duffel. "Why don't you go around back and see Evan—he should be letting the horses out to pasture. Ask him to let you into the cabin, and then he'll put you to work. I have to run into town to take care of a few things." And have a word with the bank, she thought to herself.

She was still steamed someone had been discussing her financial situation with God-knew-who, and she'd be damned before she sold the ranch to that asshole Bart Sherman. Just because his ancestors had been among the founding fathers of Rosewood didn't mean he was entitled to know everything about everyone. But he had been right. They'd been mortgage-free before Mark's accident, but when the medical bills started rolling in, she'd had no choice but to use the property as collateral to pay for them. *Shit*. Sometimes she hated living in a small town.

A short time later, after making sure six-year-old Jenna was playing happily with her dolls under Maddie Tanner's watchful eye, Sage grabbed her purse and glanced around for her keys. "Matthew, let's go! You're going to be late for practice."

Her son trudged out of his room, dragging his baseball bat behind him. His glove had been plopped on his head. From the expression on his face, one might think he was heading to the dentist for a root canal. "But Mooommm, I don't wanna go. I suck at baseball."

Sage placed her hands on her hips. "You were the one who insisted I sign you up for the summer league, so you're going. I'm not throwing away good money like that. I paid for it, and you're going." Jeez, when had she become her own mother? "Besides, you'll get better with practice—hence the reason we have to get going. We still have to swing by and get Toby."

Toby Miller was Matthew's best friend and the reason her son had wanted to join the league in the first place. His mother, Ashley, was Sage's best friend since elementary school, and the two women shared the carpooling duties for practically everything. It had been ironic they'd both fallen for men in Rosewood after growing up an hour and a half away in Saddle Brook, Oklahoma. In fact, Mark and Sage had introduced Ashley to her husband, Chris.

Reluctantly, Matthew followed her out to her five-year-old Chevy Tahoe, moaning and groaning the entire way. Sage rolled her eyes, knowing he would change his attitude when Toby climbed into the vehicle. After she heard the click of his seatbelt, she put the truck in drive.

"Mom?"

"Yes, buddy?"

"Is that man going to be working for you? The one who was in prison? Does that make him a bad man?"

Turning onto the main road, Sage sighed. How did she explain this? "Yes, Adam was in prison. He saw a man hurting a little boy, and he stopped him, but then the man got hurt. Adam took responsibility for what happened, and he went to prison. He's paid the price for hurting the man, so he's free now."

Matthew seemed to think that over for a minute. "What

happened to the other man? Did he go to prison for hurting the boy?"

"He was punished for what he did to the boy, yes." With the ultimate punishment, but her son didn't need that detail. "I want you to do me a favor, buddy. It's nobody else's business what happened to Adam in the past. He seems like a very nice man, and I don't want anyone to think he's bad because he was in prison, so can you keep that a secret?"

He shrugged. "I guess so."

"Good boy."

Sage hoped the temptation to tell one of his friends was something Matthew could resist. She knew how small towns could be with strangers in their midst. Some people might try to run Adam out of town for the "sake of our community." A few bible-thumpers came to mind.

After picking up Toby and dropping both off at the Little League field, she drove to the center of town and found a parking spot on Main Street. A quick run into the post office for some stamps was followed by selecting some new books at the library for the entire family. Sage dropped the pile on the front passenger seat of her vehicle before squaring off her shoulders and marching toward the bank. It was time to have a word with the manager, Lyle Dillinger.

The man didn't appear to be happy to see her, and the feeling was mutual, but she wasn't backing down, striding right through his open office door, bypassing his receptionist, who was on the phone. It took everything in her not to slam the door, instead shutting it with a quiet click. She crossed her arms and glared at him. "Lyle, do you mind telling me how Bart Sherman knows about me being behind in my mortgage? It's nobody else's business but mine and the bank's."

Tossing his pen on the desk he sat behind, Dillinger leaned back in his chair and gave her that superior look she'd hated for as long as she'd known him. "I have no idea how he found out, and I really don't care. What I do care about is that you are indeed behind. If you don't make several back payments soon, Sage, I'll be forced to start foreclosure proceedings."

"I told you, I have four foals being weaned within the next few weeks, and they've already been sold. As soon as they can be separated from the mothers, I'll have the money in my account and can bring my mortgage to date. All I'm asking for is a little more time."

The man sighed heavily as if she was asking him to forget the loan altogether and let her live in her home for free. She was tempted to remind him that if it weren't for Mark tutoring him, he would never have passed the social studies class needed to graduate high school. The little twit owed him a little gratitude—and since Mark was gone, she should have inherited it.

"You have until July fifteenth, Sage. Then, I'll have to go over to the courts."

The fifteenth was going to be cutting it close. If Baby Ruth's colt was weaned by then, the buyer from Texas might be willing to change the August 1st pick-up date. Another was due to be sold a few days later. The two other yearlings were going to a buyer out in California, and he planned to pick them up during a cross-country trip scheduled for the middle of August. She prayed the banker would agree to a few more days. Sage was about to give a counteroffer when the door behind her opened, and Joann Dillinger walked in. Not only was she Lyle's mother, but the statuesque woman was also the elementary school principal and one of the nicest people Sage knew—and just like that, her prayer was answered.

"Sage, darling. How nice to see you." Joann gave her a friendly hug and kiss on the cheek. "I hope I'm not interrupting. Lyle and I are going to Hilde's for lunch." The diner on Main Street was the most popular eatery in town and served amazing food for a fair price.

Not ashamed of being a little crafty and underhanded if a situation called for it, Sage smiled at the older woman. "No, Joann, you're not interrupting at all. Actually, I was just about to ask Lyle if he wouldn't mind waiting until July 22nd for me to catch up on my mortgage. That's when I'll be selling my first yearling of the season. Things have been a little tight with last year's stillborn."

Joann hoisted her purse higher on her shoulder. "Of course, Lyle will be willing to do that for you. We small-town folks have to stick together, don't we?" Out of the corner of her eye, Sage saw Lyle's frown as he rolled his eyes. But a false smile spread across his face as his mother turned to look at him. "Isn't that right, Lyle?"

"Yes, Mother, you're absolutely right." Annoyance was in his gaze as it shifted to Sage. "July twenty-second is fine. I'll see you then."

Batting her eyelashes at him, she let him know she'd won this battle between them and didn't care how she'd done it. "Thank you so much, Lyle. I'll be here bright and early on the twenty-second."

Not wanting to push her luck, she said her goodbyes and hurried out to her truck. She'd gotten a small reprieve and hoped it would be enough.

———— ❤ ————

WITH HIS GLOVED HANDS, ADAM UNROLLED THE WIRE FENCING while Evan secured it to the wooden post in the pasture at the west end of the ranch. They'd been repairing the old fence line for the past few hours, and Adam had removed his T-shirt a short time after they'd started. He wasn't used to the high Oklahoma temperatures yet, having spent most of the time since his release in the cooler, northern states during the spring. It wasn't even summer yet, and the fore-casters predicted the season would be hotter than normal —if today were a clear indication, they were probably right.

Earlier, they'd patched the barn's roof where the storm that'd blown through yesterday had ripped off a few shin-gles. After that, they'd come out here to take care of the fence. Glancing to his left, Adam noted they had three more posts to go. The ranch's border collie, Benji, was taking a break from keeping the sheep and llamas grouped together, away from the temporary opening in the fence, and was resting in the shade of the pick-up truck the men were using.

The ranch foreman worked beside Adam silently, which didn't bother him at all—in fact, it was a content camaraderie they'd found together. Quiet was something Adam had missed a great deal while in prison. Even in the dead of night, there had still been noises of the guards walking around, doors opening and closing, and any number of men moving around in their cells, snoring, or talking in their sleep. After his release, Adam had discov-ered his new-found silence at night could be louder than a bomb going off, and it had taken him a while to get used to it.

When Evan had approached Adam on the porch a few hours ago, he'd posed a few questions about his background, which was completely understood—after all, he was a stranger in town. During his odd jobs here and there, Adam had been selective on how much he divulged about himself. If the job was a day or two of hard labor before moving on, it hadn't been necessary to fill his temporary employer in on his past. There had been a few people he'd met whom he'd felt comfortable sharing personal info with, but not many—and certainly not all the details. He didn't know why he'd come right out and told Sage, then Evan, about his incarceration and how it'd come about, but it'd felt like the right thing to do. The foreman had said he would've responded to the situation in the same manner, although he couldn't swear the man's death would have been an accident. Adam thought the man had exaggerated, but one never knew how far they would truly go unless they faced the evil in person.

While on top of the barn, Evan had filled him in about the ranch history and how it'd been in Mark Hammond's family for several generations. Two and a half years ago, Mark had taken one of the horses up the ridge on the north end of the property, something he did several times a week, but an hour later, the horse had returned without its rider. Sage and Evan raced out to find Mark, who'd been discovered on one of the trails—he'd been thrown by the horse, striking his head on a rock. The critically injured man had lived another week in a coma while never regaining consciousness. Ultimately, Sage decided to pull the plug on his life support and donate his organs after the doctors had finally declared he was brain dead. Adam couldn't imagine how hard that had been on her, especially with their two young children.

"That should do it for today." Evan removed his straw cowboy hat and wiped his face with a bandana he'd pulled from his pocket. The fifty-nine-year-old man was in excellent shape for his age, but his skin was weathered from his years working in the sun. "By the time we put everything away and wash up, it'll be dinner time."

"Sounds good to me. If your wife's dinner is as good as her breakfast, I would say you're a very lucky man."

"Oh, I'm a very lucky man, indeed, and it has more to do with just Maddie's cooking. She was my elementary school sweetheart, believe it or not. I think I fell in love with her when I was eight years old, and she hit a home run off me at recess. There's been no other woman for me ever since."

Adam laughed as they loaded the tools and leftover material into the bed of the pick-up. "Love at first bat, huh?"

The older man grinned. "Something like that, yeah."

After Benji jumped into the bed, Adam flipped the tailgate up, then rounded to the passenger door and climbed in. Evan started the truck and put it in Drive. Mulling over what had occurred that morning, Adam decided to ask about it. "What's with that rancher, Bart, whatever-his-name-is? I spotted you in the background with the shotgun. Expecting trouble?"

The older man snorted. "Well, honestly, the shotgun was for you after I noticed you walking up to the house. Can't be too careful these days." Adam nodded his agreement. "But Bart Sherman is a different kind of trouble altogether. He's been after the Hammond property for years, wanting to buy it from Mark, but there was no way that boy would've sold it—to Bart or anybody else. Mark was born and raised here—he loved this land, and I don't blame him. Either you're a rancher, or you're not. It's a tough life at times and not for everybody."

"So, Bart is just looking to expand his own ranch?"

"I guess so. He's got the three hundred acres on the other side of that fence we were working on. Cattle rancher."

"Hmm. Will Sage be okay, or is selling something she'll have to consider?" He hoped not. "I don't know much about ranching, but from what I've heard, more owners than not are struggling to survive."

"It's been rough. She had to take out a mortgage to pay Mark's medical bills—it'll be a few years before she can finish paying it off. And last year, one of the foals was still-born, putting a crimp in the ranch's annual income. But if all goes well, and there are no big expenses that pop up this year, Sage should be okay."

Evan parked the vehicle next to the barn and glanced at his watch. "The stuff can stay in the truck since we need to work on some more of the fence line on Monday. Sundays around here are basic chores only—been that way since Mark's folks first took over the place. If you want to go wash up, dinner will be at five-thirty. Just let yourself into the kitchen through the back-porch door."

Thirty minutes later, Adam approached the main house, fresh from a well-needed shower, wearing a clean T-shirt and jeans. Drifting from town to town, he only had work clothes with him and one pair of nice pants and a button-down white shirt for church every week. It didn't matter which church he attended as long as it was based on the Christian faith, and over the past few months, he'd enjoyed a variety of denominations. Reverend Stevens' church was Protestant, and Adam had liked the man instantly when he'd met him outside the building early this morning after being dropped off by a trucker he'd hitched a ride from.

Climbing the back steps, Adam knocked on the wood frame of the screen door. The aromas of savory meat and freshly baked bread assaulted his sense of smell, causing his stomach to growl and his mouth to water.

"Come on in!" a female voice called to him.

Pulling open the door, he stepped inside a cheery, yellow kitchen and was greeted by a round, petite, dark-haired tornado of a woman flitting about the room. "Hi, there. You must be Adam. I'm Maddie, and it's nice to meet you. Knocking isn't necessary in my kitchen. Just walk right in."

She handed him a heaping bowl of mashed potatoes and a filled gravy boat, then pointed behind him. "Would you mind putting these on the dining room table? I'll be right behind you with the roast."

He couldn't help the grin that spread across his face at her peppiness. "Absolutely. And it's nice to meet you, too, ma'am."

Turning in the direction she'd indicated, he almost ran into Evan, who was returning from dropping other dishes on the long, wooden table. Stepping out of the way, Adam let the older man pass before continuing into the dining room. The only other person there was Sage's son. The boy looked at him with curiosity but remained quiet. Adam set the dishes down in the middle of the table. "Matthew, right?" The child nodded. "That's a good strong name. It means 'gift of God.'"

"It was my grandfather's name," Matthew stated with a proud smile. He had his mother's bow-shaped mouth and hazel eyes, but his light blond hair had to have come from his father, whom Adam noticed in a family photo hanging on the wall. "I'm named after him. He was the best, but he's gone now."

"I'm sorry to hear that, but we have something in common then. I'm also named after my grandfather, but I never knew him. He's been gone a long time too." He held out his hand. "My name is Adam, and it's nice to meet you, Matthew."

The boy shook his hand with a nice strong grip for such a young boy. "It's nice to meet you too. What does Adam mean?"

"Man of the earth."

"Huh." He paused a moment, clearly thinking about something. "What does Mark mean? That's my dad's name."

"Hmm. If I remember correctly, I think it means 'war-like.'"

Matthew's brow furrowed. "A warlock? Like a man witch?"

Laughing, Adam shook his head—his New York accent was causing problems again. "No. Not a warlock. War-like. It means . . . he was a brave warrior." The definition was a bit of a stretch, but he didn't want the kid to think his father was belligerent or hostile, as the definition of the word suggested.

"That's so cool!"

"What's cool?"

Adam and the boy turned their heads to see Sage walk in from the living room with a shy-looking little girl who seemed intimidated at the sight of him. She popped her thumb in her mouth and stepped closer to her mother. From the kitchen, Maddie and Evan came with the last of the dishes of food.

"Dad was a brave warrior," Matthew exclaimed. "Adam says that's what 'Mark' means."

Sage guided her daughter to a chair next to Matthew before taking a seat at the head of the table. "Really? That is pretty cool. Please, Adam, take a seat." She gestured to the chair at the opposite end of the table from her as Evan and Maddie sat across from the children.

"What does Jenna mean? That's my sister's name." The curious boy pointed at the little girl beside him, but Adam had already learned her name.

"Matthew, that's enough," Sage chastised. "Adam doesn't want to answer a bunch of questions during his dinner."

Adam smiled. "It's okay, but Jenna is not one of the names I'm familiar with, so maybe we can look it up later."

A slight frown crossed Sage's face, and Adam wondered if he'd overstepped his boundaries—after all, he was an employee who'd just been hired a few hours ago.

Sage held her hands out toward her daughter and Maddie. "Matthew, please say grace."

Everyone joined hands as the boy bowed his head. "Please, God, bless our food, our family, and our ranch. Bless all our friends and give Daddy a hug for us and . . . and . . . oh, yeah, bless our animals too. Amen."

"Amen," the rest chorused.

It wasn't long before plates were filled, and everyone was enjoying the meal. Conversations about various topics flowed on both the adult and juvenile levels, and Adam found the family pleasant and entertaining. The only person who didn't speak to him was six-year-old Jenna. However, she did give him a few shy smiles before whispering something to her mother, who would repeat the question or statement loudly enough for the others to hear.

Apparently, Jenna's shyness around new people was not to be misconstrued as her being rude. Having been a youth advisor in the Brotherhood, Adam decided to try and engage her in conversation, hoping she would feel more at ease with him. "Jenna, Benji told me the funniest jokes today. Would you like to hear them?"

Her eyes widened as she glanced from him to the dog sleeping under her chair and back to him again. Slowly, she dipped her chin once.

"What animal keeps the best time?"

Shrugging her shoulders, she swallowed a mouthful of mashed potatoes.

"A watchdog."

As Jenna's grin appeared once more, Matthew laughed boisterously.

Okay, it's a start. Try one more. "Why do you need a license for a dog and not for a cat?"

Another shrug.

"Because cats can't drive."

This time a giggle emerged, and she covered her mouth with a little hand. "That's thilly. Dogth can't drive, either."

Her little lisp from a missing front tooth was adorable. Raising his eyebrows, Adam pretended to be stunned. "Really? Then tell Benji because he's the one who told me the joke."

"Dogth can't talk." She laughed harder, the sweet melody warming his heart.

"All animals can talk—you just have to understand their language."

"Like Dr. Doolittle," Matthew exclaimed.

"Exactly." Adam's gaze met Sage's across the table, and he was relieved to see she was smiling in approval—two positive results for two silly jokes—not bad. From that point on, Jenna became as much a chatterbox as her older brother, and Adam had a fun time entertaining them both.

After the table had been cleared and the women shooed the men out of the kitchen so they could do the dishes, Evan took Adam out to the barn to show him how to feed the horses their second meal of the day. By the time the chores were all done, Adam couldn't wait to hit his pillow. Working outdoors in the fresh air was a suggestion he had for anyone suffering from insomnia because it sure did help him get a good night's sleep.

Chapter Four

After tucking her children into bed, Sage checked the locks on the front door before cutting through the kitchen to the backdoor. When she'd been a young child, small-town residents never locked their doors, but times had changed, and she felt safer knowing the house was secure, especially since Mark had died. Even though Evan and Maddie's cabin was only about a football field to the east of the main house, it was still far enough away that someone could break in and remain unnoticed by the older couple.

Swinging the screen door open, she stepped out onto the back porch and descended the stairs. She wanted to do a walk through the barn to check on the horses before climbing into bed herself. The three nursing mares would start weaning their yearlings soon, and the six pregnant ones would be going into labor within the next week or so. Hopefully, this year's births would all be healthy. Last year's stillborn had been a financial disappointment, in addition to being a sad lesson in life and death for Sage's children, who loved to watch the foals being born.

It'd been a long day, and her feet were killing her. After her errands in town, she'd returned to the Little League field to wait for the boys' practice to be finished. Unfortunately, that meant she had to deal with Seth Chapman—divorced father of three kids of whom he had partial custody, avid drinker, and, according to him, God's gift to women everywhere. Little did he know, his crassness, pot belly, and yellowing teeth from tobacco chewing begged to differ with that opinion. The man had been hitting on Sage since the month after Mark had died and still couldn't get it through his thick skull that she had absolutely no interest in him.

When she'd finally driven Toby home, she'd chatted with Ashley for a few minutes while the boys played with the new barn kittens. At first, her friend had been happy Sage found someone to help around the ranch, but as soon as she mentioned Adam's past, Sage knew she'd made a mistake.

"Are you crazy? A criminal? Sage, how could you hire an ex-con? What was he in for?"

She bit her tongue. Even though she loved her best friend, Ashley tended to be a bit of a blabbermouth at times. She knew Ash didn't mean to gossip as much as she did, but occasionally her brain-to-mouth filter was broken. "I'd rather not say. It's in his past, and he's paid his debt to society. Everyone deserves a second chance, right? Besides, he was upfront about everything and told me to call a few people to make sure he was being honest. I did, and they gave him glowing references. He even won over Reverend Stevens and Evan."

Ash raised her brow. "Really? Evan is more protective of you and the kids than Mark was, and that's saying a lot.

Okay. I understand that you don't want his background to get out, but please just be careful and sleep with your gun under your pillow. Second chances or not, I would hate to see anything happen to you or the kids."

After making sure none of the pregnant mares were in labor, Sage scratched a few noses on her way out of the barn. Shutting the big red door, she glanced over at the little two-room cabin, which sat a few yards away. The lights were still on inside, and she pivoted in that direction, telling herself she would just check and see if Adam needed anything. At dinner earlier, he'd said the cabin appeared to have everything, but she wanted to make sure.

As she approached, she noticed the curtains were open in the front living room. The bedroom and bath were at the rear of the structure. Not wanting to disturb him if he'd fallen asleep with the lights on—Evan had said the younger man had worked his ass off during the day—she peeked through the window.

Well, he definitely wasn't asleep. Dressed in a pair of black sweatpants and nothing more, Adam was kneeling in profile on the floor with his hands resting on his muscular thighs and his head tilted down. His eyes were shut, and she guessed he was meditating. Staying in the shadows, she studied his features—dark-blond hair in need of a slight trim, a chiseled jaw covered in coarse stubble, corded neck muscles, broad shoulders and chest, followed by a narrow waist and rock-hard abs. A deep V of muscles, dusted with fine hair down the middle, disappeared into his sweatpants.

Holy crap, is it getting hot out here?

She may be a widow, who was still mourning the only man she'd ever loved, but she would have to be six feet under along with Mark not to appreciate the perfect male form in front of her.

A stirring developed deep in her womb, and she felt her panties grow damp. For the first time since Mark's death, Sage felt a longing and desire. Her nipples tightened as her mouth watered.

Shit!

Why did it have to be this man who brought her libido out of its thirty-month slumber? She'd felt something earlier after he'd caught her smiling at how he'd gotten Jenna talking at dinner. There was something about the way his eyes seemed to dance while his deep, rumbling laughter filled the air, and, jeez, his dimples were just too adorable.

Stop it. Stop thinking about him as a man. He's your employee and nothing more.

He probably wouldn't be here for long, and one-night stands weren't her thing. And there was no way she was having a meaningless fling one-hundred-and-fifty feet from where her children were sleeping soundly. But, damn, she was lonely. It wasn't a new feeling or one she'd been denying to herself, but it wasn't something she'd acted on. She missed being held, caressed, and loved. Maybe Ashley was right—her friend had spent the past six months trying to convince Sage it was okay to start dating again. Maybe it was time to rejoin the living in every way.

Adam's chin dipped, and it wasn't until he made the sign of the cross that she realized he'd been praying. He'd mentioned he wanted to attend church—she was a member of Reverend Stevens' congregation as well—but she wasn't used to seeing anyone pray like that outside of Sunday service or the dinner table.

Suddenly embarrassed she'd been ogling him, she

stepped further into the shadows as Adam stood and stretched. With one last admiring glance at the man, she spun on her heel and hurried back to her house, completely forgetting what she'd been doing outside of the cottage in the first place.

Closing and locking the kitchen door behind her, Sage leaned against it with a sigh and subconsciously fingered the gold wedding ring still adorning her left hand. She had to be out of her mind. Adam was an employee . . . an ex-con employee . . . a drifting, ex-con employee, whom she had just met this morning. There . . . now that she had that straight in her mind, she could push away the thoughts of his amazing physique and how her own body had reacted at the sight. *Damn.*

———— ♥ ————

MAKING THE SIGN OF THE CROSS AT THE END OF HIS MEDITATION and prayers, Adam pushed himself to his feet and winced as his knees cracked. At some point recently, he'd noticed his body was showing signs of aging. Forty was rapidly approaching, and every one of those years seemed to be making themselves known of late—the cracking of his joints, a dull ache in his lower back, some gray hairs at his temples, and a few wrinkles on his face which hadn't been there before.

Movement out the cabin's front window caught his eye, and he watched Sage climb the few steps to the back porch, enter her home, and turn off the exterior light. A few seconds passed, and then the kitchen went dark as well.

Stepping over to the window, Adam stared out at the

darkness that was now only illuminated by the sliver of moon overhead. He crossed his arms over his bare chest and leaned against the frame molding. While it had been hot for the entire day, as soon as the sun had gone down, so had the temperature. Instead of turning on the two air conditioning units, which were installed in wall cut-outs in this room and his bedroom, he'd left the windows open earlier, allowing the fresh air to permeate the small cabin. Before he'd started his meditation, he'd closed them again due to the chill.

What am I doing here, Lord? Is this just another temporary stop in my journey, or is there a reason you led me here?

Something had made him take a left at a fork in the road instead of a right. Something had told him to head south instead of any other direction. Something had made all those cars and trucks drive by the lone male hitchhiker instead of picking him up. Something had told that retired couple it was safe to offer him a ride on their way to Texas via Oklahoma to see their new grandson. And something had made him thank them several hours later before taking his duffel bag and throwing it onto his back again when they'd stopped for gas. The exit ramp they'd taken for the service station had dumped them on County Road 81, which, if one went west on it, led directly into downtown Rosewood, five miles away. A trucker had picked him up about halfway there and dropped him off in front of Reverend Stevens's church, and something had made the good reverend think he could help a widow in need. He wasn't sure what all those *somethings* were, but he'd been drawn here as if this was where he belonged. There had been so many crapshoot decisions made by him and others and had just one of them made a different choice, he never would be standing here contemplating his pretty new boss and her two adorable children.

Am I here to help Sage save her ranch? Or is there more to it?

He couldn't deny the attraction he'd felt toward her from the moment she'd confronted him outside her home. She was a strong woman—standing up to Sherman and his "guard dog" had proven that immediately—but she was also a soft woman who still mourned the loss of her husband. And Adam was a man who hadn't even held a woman's hand since he'd been a teenager unless it had been to comfort one in a time of need.

The thought of Sage's womanly curves had him twitching in his sweatpants. He was no longer in the Brotherhood, but that didn't mean he wasn't still faithful to his God. Temptation had been something he'd faced many times since he'd taken his vows. Temptations of the flesh had ranked at the top of the list. He wouldn't be human if they weren't.

Since his release from prison, he'd been adjusting to not only the fact he was a legally and physically free man but also emotionally and mentally. There had been several women who'd flirted with him during his travels these past few months, and although he'd been flattered, being with any of them in the biblical sense hadn't felt right. Yes, it could have been a release of a lot of pent-up sexual energy for him, but there was still a part of him that felt a man and a woman shouldn't lie together unless they were in love. The older brothers and clergymen from other faiths would argue that a couple had to be married before they had intercourse, but times had changed over the many centuries since those religious "laws" had been written. As long as someone didn't harm another in any manner and did what they could to help others, leniencies could be allowed.

But he *had* harmed another, and that act still darkened his soul, despite the extenuating circumstances. A man had died at his hand, and while he hoped God would forgive him come his Judgment Day, he wasn't sure he could ever forgive himself.

Pushing off from the window frame, Adam strode across the cabin to his bedroom. It was a step above sparse, with a few basic impersonal touches about the room. But a lack of worldly possessions was something he'd gotten used to in both the seminary and rectories he'd lived in for almost two decades and the six-by-eight-foot cell that had been his home for over five years.

Flopping down on the full-sized bed, he picked up the worn, paperback copy of a John Grisham novel he'd gotten at a yard sale for $.25 a few days ago in a small town in Iowa, as he'd been heading out toward the interstate to hitch a ride. Only a few pages into the book, his eyes felt heavy. Unable to fight falling asleep any longer, he switched off the bedside lamp and rolled onto his side, finding a comfortable spot on the pillow under his head. His last conscious thought as slumber overtook him was Sage Hammond really was a beautiful woman.

———— ❤ ————

GROANING, ADAM ROLLED OVER AND STRETCHED OUT A FEW kinks. It was day fourteen of working at the Heaven's Pasture Ranch, and he slept better every night, followed by a run each morning before breakfast. During his time in prison, he'd kept up his physical fitness as best he could, but there had been few aerobic activities, so his workouts consisted mostly of weights and Krav Maga Retzev drills. Those consisted of practicing strike after strike at an intended target in continual motion until the threat was eliminated, and while they got his heart rate up, Adam had missed his morning runs. Since his release, he'd worked himself back up to four miles per day. Combining that with the physical labor required to keep a ranch running and in good condition, he started feeling fitter than he had in years.

The only thing bothering him physically now was his continuing reaction to his dreams about one Ms. Sage Hammond. Having erections was a normal bodily function for any healthy male, but after taking a vow of celibacy, he'd resorted to meditation to overcome them. That had changed in prison. He'd quickly learned that any hard-on, brought on by any reason, made a person a target for sexual assault. So, masturbation became a part of his life again—something he hadn't done since he'd been a teenager—but it'd taken him a while to stop feeling guilty about it.

Standing, he headed to the small bathroom. Just as he flushed the toilet, a pounding on the cabin's front door startled him.

"Adam! Adam! Hurry! Come quick!"

Matthew sounded frantic and breathless. Yanking on his sweatpants, Adam rushed to the door and swung it open. "What's wrong?"

The boy's face was lit up like it was Christmas morning. "Diamond Lil is having her baby! You have to come watch it with us!" He grabbed Adam's hand and tried to pull him outside.

"Okay. Okay. Hang on. Let me get my shirt and shoes."

Hastily dressing, he chuckled at Matthew's impatience. He was shifting back and forth on the balls of his feet,

45

gesturing with his hands for Adam to get dressed faster. "Hurry, or we'll miss it!"

A few moments later, he followed the boy into the barn, where Sage, Jenna, and Evan were peering into a stall. Sage smiled at him, and he felt a renewed stirring in his groin. Without makeup and her hair pulled up in a loose ponytail, she was prettier than any woman he'd ever met. Her hazel eyes danced with excitement as she waved him over. "You're just in time. She went into labor sometime after I checked on her last night around nine-thirty."

Adam stepped over to see the white and black spotted mare lying on a bed of hay. Her nostrils flared as her body quivered with a contraction. Sweat glistened off her coat.

Glancing at the faces of the children and their mother, Adam grinned. This was obviously something they'd all witnessed before and had been anticipating for weeks.

Jenna looked up at him. "Have you ever theen a baby horthe being born, Adam?"

"No, Little Bird, I haven't." He'd looked up the meaning of her name after their first dinner together and used it as a nickname ever since. It fit her to a "T" with her sweet voice and constant chattering now that she was comfortable around him. "But I did see a cat have kittens once when I was about Matthew's age."

"Our barn cat had kittenth before, but a baby horthe is even better!"

"Really? How come? I thought all babies were special."

She held out her hands as if the answer should be obvious to him. "Becauthe the baby kittenth can't do anything until they get bigger, but a baby horthe can thand thoon after being born."

Beside him, Sage chuckled and leaned toward him. "Can't argue with that logic, can you?"

He laughed along with her. "No, I guess I can't."

"Look," Evan announced. "Here come the front hooves."

Sure enough, the newborn was making its entrance into the world. After much snorting and straining from Diamond Lil and several contractions later, the filly slid from the womb with a final gush of amniotic fluid to the soft cheers of the small crowd watching. She was a beautiful animal, mostly white, with splashes of black on her nose and hindquarters. The relieved mare began to clean her baby.

From where she stood behind him, Sage put her hands on Matthew's shoulders. "Okay, buddy. It's your turn to name her. Did you decide which name you wanted from the list we made?"

"Uh-huh. Since today is Tuesday, I'm going to call her Ruby Tuesday."

Adam grinned at Sage. "A Rolling Stones fan, huh?"

"My dad was a big fan, so I grew up listening to every album they made." She tilted her head in the direction of the house. "Come on. Maddie came over to cook breakfast a little early after I called Evan about the foal."

He looked down at his thrown-on attire. His run could wait until this evening before dinner. "Sure. Just give me ten minutes to clean up, and I'll be right over."

"Okay."

After giving Jenna a wink and ruffling Matthew's hair, Adam hurried back to his cabin. He quickly made himself more presentable for the day and pulled on the old pair of cowboy boots he'd found at a thrift shop in town following Sunday services. The Tanners and Hammonds attended the same church, but they couldn't fit everyone into one vehicle, so he'd hitched a ride with Sage and her kids. Evan had been right—Sundays were quiet on the ranch aside from caring for the animals. Maddie had made roasted chicken for an early repast, then Adam and Evan retired to the back porch for a chess game. The older man was good, and his strategies had Adam scratching his head a few times.

When he entered the kitchen, Maddie handed him a heaping plate of pancakes and bacon sans the grits. Try as he may, he still couldn't acquire a taste for them. Taking a seat at the dining room table, he thanked Sage as she placed a mug of coffee next to his plate. As he added cream and sugar, he glanced at her as she sat at the other end of the table. Evan and the children were missing and probably still out in the barn with the newborn.

"So, what's on the agenda today?" he asked. "Evan mentioned he and Maddie were riding to Oklahoma City for some supplies and told me to see what you wanted me to work on today." It was a four-hour round trip to the big city for the couple, and they made it every six weeks or so. Maddie had family there, so they tended to make a full day out of it.

"Well, Jenna is going with them to visit Maddie's great-niece, who is her age. And Matthew's friend invited him over for the day to go swimming, so it's just you and me. I was thinking of taking a ride up the ridge after taking care of the animals. Want to come with me?"

"A 'ride' like in the truck or on a horse?"

She chuckled. "Don't tell me you don't know how to ride a horse."

"Well, I could," he replied sheepishly, "but then I'd be lying. Actually, I did go riding once when I was fourteen. It was the first year with the foster parents, who I'd lived with for the rest of my teens. There were four of us, I think, at the time, and a cop who Harry worked with, his family had a dude ranch in upstate New York. We went for a long weekend, and while I had fun, I remember how much my thighs and rear hurt afterward."

"Ha! Yeah, there is that. But if I promise not to let the horses take off at a gallop and supply the Tylenol when it's over, would you like to go for a ride? I could teach you." A light blush appeared on her cheeks, and her gaze dropped to the floor. "I mean if you want. You don't have to if you don't want to."

Her sudden shyness was endearing, but he liked her smile even better. "I'd love to. Besides, what good is a ranch hand if he doesn't know how to ride, right?"

He got the response he wanted. A smile. "Um, right."

The kitchen door swung open, and the kids came running in, chattering about the new filly. Evan was right behind them. Soon everyone was digging into breakfast, and it was another few hours before Adam and Sage found themselves alone in the barn. She placed the reins on two horses and led them out to a hitching post as Adam followed her.

"What's this big guy's name?" He stroked the animal's strong, elegant neck. Its brown coat was offset by a white chest and a similar patch on its right hindquarter. "He's a beauty."

"And he knows it. That's Othello, and this is Topaz." She scratched the other horse's nose before starting back into the barn. "I have to grab one of Mark's old saddles up in the loft."

He followed. "I can get it for you."

Sage stepped over to the built-in ladder. "Actually, it's probably easier if I hand it down to you."

"You're the boss."

Laughing, she climbed and disappeared into the loft. "And don't you forget it." It took a moment before she reappeared at the edge and carefully lowered the brown leather saddle into his waiting hands. He placed it to the side on the ground and turned to make sure Sage descended safely. She was halfway down the ladder when her foot slipped, and his stomach dropped as he lunged for her.

Chapter Five

S age had no idea why she'd invited Adam along for the
ride she usually took alone. When Mark was alive,
she'd occasionally accompanied him on his treks through
the woods or set out on her own as he did sometimes.
They'd loved to spend time alone together, but they also
knew the other needed some time just by themselves. It
was a form of ranch therapy for them——a way to destress
when things got hectic.

This would be the first time she'd be taking someone
with her since Mark had died. Her thoughts briefly went
back to that horrible day. She had been having one of those
days where everything and everyone seemed to aggravate
her. He'd offered to saddle up her horse for her to go riding
with him, and she turned him down to catch up on the
laundry, of all things. It was a decision she would regret for
the rest of her life, but she'd finally learned to stop playing
the "what-if" game. What if she'd gone with him? Would
he still be alive? That question would never be answered,
and about a year and a half ago, she stopped wondering. To
put it to rest, she wrote the question on a piece of paper and

stuck it in a small hole she'd dug in his grave. For some reason, that had been the day she'd officially buried Mark in her mind and started making plans for the future without him. But it hadn't extended to every part of her life. She still wore her wedding band, unable to bring herself to remove it.

Over the last few days, she'd grown more curious and attracted to her new ranch hand. He was a handsome man, polite, great with her kids, and generally a nice person with a great sense of humor. They'd enjoyed a cup of coffee together the past few nights, sitting out on the back porch after the kids had gone to sleep—they'd alternated between general conversations and periods of comfortable silence. She was even getting over the fact he had been in prison, especially since she didn't think he'd deserved to be there in the first place. What kind of man would plead guilty to manslaughter, when he most likely could've gotten off scot-free, just to keep a child from having to testify? A man with a very big heart, in her mind.

Up in the loft, she pulled the small tarp off Mark's old saddle and ran her fingertips over the well-worn leather. Five years ago, with the help of Maddie, she'd used as many coupons as she could to scrimp and save to buy it for her husband on his thirtieth birthday. To say he'd been shocked was an understatement.

Shaking off the old memories, she lifted the saddle and carried it to the loft's edge. Handing the saddle down to Adam, Sage tried to tell herself this wasn't a date they were on, just two new friends—scratch that—an employer and employee spending a few hours together. All she was doing was taking him for a tour of the rest of her property he hadn't seen yet.

Then why the hell was her gaze focused on his full lips

every time he spoke, wanting to know what it would be like if he kissed her?

Turning, she began her descent back down the ladder. She was halfway down when her foot slipped, and she felt herself falling. A startled screech escaped her as two strong male arms wrapped around her torso. But Adam had also been caught off guard, and now they were both tumbling to the ground. He hit the floor first, and she landed right on top of him. A hushed "*oomph*" came from beneath her.

Twisting in his arms, she grabbed his shoulders. "Oh, my God, Adam! Are you all right?"

His hands cupped her cheeks, his eyes searching her face frantically. "I-I'm fine. Are you okay?"

"Yes. I'm good. I'm so sorry." She was suddenly aware of their positioning. Her hips were flush against his as their legs were tangled together. Her breath caught as she saw his soft brown eyes fill with heat, and she felt his cock twitch between them. She licked her lips, and his gaze zoomed in on the action. More and more, over the past few days, her attraction to him had grown, despite her intent to ignore it. But now, unable to resist her longing for this man anymore, she lowered her head and brushed her lips to his.

Adam's body tensed, and he let out a low groan before returning the chaste kiss. While he wasn't a horrible kisser, he seemed hesitant. His lips were soft on the surface, but she felt their hidden power, which he was clearly holding back. When he didn't deepen the kiss, she pulled a few inches away, and their eyes met. "You don't have to be gentle, you know. I won't break."

The man blushed . . . actually, flat-out blushed. "I'm not sure I remember how to kiss a woman. It's been a long time."

Of course! He'd been in prison for over five years and

probably hadn't been with a woman in the short time he'd been out. "Five years is a long time, but it's like riding a bike." She ground her hips against his and was pleased to see his eyes roll back a little as the bulge in his pants grew.

His hands skimmed up and down her arms, and he cleared his throat. "Actually . . . uh . . . it's . . . uh . . . been closer to twenty years."

What? Oh, my God! She scrambled off him and jumped to her feet. How could she have been so stupid and misread things? "I'm so sorry. I had no idea you were gay."

His eyes flashed wide. "What! No . . . no, I'm not gay." He chuckled, then winced as he stood and shifted his hips. "Definitely not gay."

She stared at him in confusion. "Then I don't understand. Why haven't you kissed a woman in almost twenty years?"

Adam took a deep breath and ran a hand through his hair. Pieces of straw separated from the strands and fell to the floor. "Because I was a celibate friar."

Friar? That was like a monk, wasn't it?

Her mouth dropped, and then she started laughing. Oh, Lord, the man was funny. She hadn't been this entertained since Mark was alive.

"I'm not kidding, Sage."

Her laughter died at his serious expression. *Oh. My. God.* She felt the blood drain from her face. *What have I just done?*

"I became a Franciscan Brother at twenty-one, but I started my studies—and my celibacy—two years before that."

Sage's mouth opened and closed several times before her thoughts managed to get from her brain to her tongue. "Are you . . . are you telling me you're a vir-virgin?"

"Ha!" He shook his head with a wry expression. "Um. Not exactly. I had a few experiences with two girls I'd dated. One in high school and the other during my first year of college before I felt a higher calling and enrolled in the seminary." His blush deepened again. "But those times were a bit juvenile and experimental . . . and a really long time ago."

Stunned, she was so embarrassed and couldn't look him in the eye. While Mark had been her first and only lover, she was far from naïve. But Adam was as inexperienced as a teenager. Oh, Lord, he must think she was some sort of slut for jumping him like that. "I'm so sorry. I had no idea. I never would have kissed you if I had known you were a monk . . . I mean, a friar."

Were they even the same thing?

Stepping toward her, he used his hand to lift her chin until their gazes met once more. "Please don't be sorry. I enjoyed it—very much. Before I started my prison sentence, I resigned from the order. Between what I had done and why I had done it, I felt I couldn't be committed to the Brotherhood anymore. But my celibacy has never been a problem for me . . . until now. I'm attracted to you, Sage. I can't deny that—and more than just physically. I'm just not sure what I'm supposed to do here. Can we take this slowly?"

"Um . . . sure. I just . . ." She blew out a shaky breath—one which matched her quivering knees. "I just want you to know that . . . um . . . I'm not normally like this . . . forward, I mean."

Crap. Now she was the one who sounded like a teenager. Her cheeks warmed, and she twined her fingers together, uncertain of what else to do with them. "I'm not usually forward with a man. I mean, Mark was the only man I'd ever been with, and there hasn't been anyone else since."

He gave her a shy smile, causing those dimples she liked so much to reappear. "So, you don't mind taking things slow and seeing where they lead us?"

Her head bobbed a few times. "Not at all. Slow sounds good . . . and nice."

"Yes, it does." He leaned down and skimmed his soft lips across hers before straightening again. "It sounds very nice."

Carrying the saddle outside, Adam placed it on Othello's back and followed Sage's instructions on how to secure it to the animal. Once that was complete, she gave him a few pointers on how to mount and ride—doing so helped push away the last of her embarrassment. It seemed to have the same effect on him. After she'd covered all the basics, he planted his foot in the stirrup and swung his other leg over the majestic beast, settling into the leather seat.

"Not bad," Sage praised as she mounted her own horse, trying to ignore how good he looked perched atop Othello. "You ready?"

"As I'll ever be . . . I guess."

She chuckled. "You'll do fine. Just don't let go of the reins." She eyed his clenched hands. "And relax a little."

"Easy for you to say."

Giving Topaz's sides a light tap with her heels, Sage led the way around the barn, heading out toward Eagle's Ridge. While most of the land belonging to Heaven's Pastures was flat and perfect for grazing, the property lines extended a fair distance up the ridge. She usually let Topaz run the expanse before they reached the tree line, but with Adam's inexperience, that was out of the question today. It took them about fifteen minutes at a comfortable walk to reach the bottom of the ridge, where the ground began a steady incline. Staying on the path that had been created decades ago, the horses trod single file until the trail widened a little and they could walk shoulder to shoulder again.

"How're you doing, Adam?" Sage glanced at him. He'd visibly relaxed during the steady ride out and seemed much more comfortable with his mount than when he'd first gotten on.

"Well, Othello hasn't thrown me to the dirt yet, so I guess I'm doing okay."

Sage grimaced but stayed quiet. Othello was the horse Mark had been riding the day of his accident—the horse had returned to the barn without him.

"It's beautiful up here. Do you ride through the woods often?"

Pulling a bottle of water from her saddle bag, she handed it to him before grabbing another for herself. While it was cooler here among the trees, the temperatures were still in the low nineties. Hopefully, the rain that was predicted for tonight would knock it down a few degrees. "Not as often as I would like. But I try to come up at least once a week. It's my time to forget I'm a mother and ranch owner with all the stress those things involved. I get to clear my mind and relax. Some women go to day spas . . . I come up here."

"I like your style. Although, I get the feeling I'll wish for a day spa when I'm hurting tonight."

She pointed in front of them. "There's a small, spring-fed lake about ten minutes from here. We'll take a break there." She grinned. "If you can make it that far, New York."

A smirk spread across his face. "You're on, Oklahoma. Lead the way."

When they finally approached the lake, movement caught her attention, and she pulled on the reins. Beside her, Adam did the same, bringing Othello to a halt. "What's wrong?"

"Look." She pointed to the edge of the water. A deer and two small fawns were taking a drink. The mother lifted her head at the sound of Sage's voice, but after realizing there was no threat, she leaned down to the water again. "That's why I love coming up here. I've always loved animals . . . big, small, cute, ugly . . . any and all."

"I could tell when you watched the foal being born this morning. Your eyes were dancing as much as the kids' were. It's easy to see where they get it from."

Sage blushed—why, she didn't know. Maybe it was just that he'd noticed how much she loved watching the birth.

Leaving the momma and her fawns alone, Sage led Adam further around the lake before stopping and dismounting. She stifled a laugh when he groaned and stretched. She might have to give him tomorrow off since they still had the ride back.

Taking the reins of both horses, she led them to the water's edge so they could drink. The sounds of nature surrounded them—the small waterfall fed by the underground spring from further up the ridge, the calls of the different birds, and the rustling of a small unseen animal running through the brush. Sage could stay here all day.

"What are you thinking about?"

Startled, her gaze met Adam's. "Why?"

He grinned. "Because you had this faraway look in your eyes, and you were smiling at something I couldn't see."

Shrugging, she took the saddle bag off Othello and sat on a large flat rock. "Nothing really—just how much I love it up here. Believe it or not, this is still Hammond property, but I'm not exactly sure why they bought it back in the eighteen-hundreds or kept it over the years. It's not farmable or useful for any reason. Well, maybe that's why it still belongs to us because who the heck is going to buy it from us other than the government, and they'll just make it into a state park." She moved over to give him room to join her while pulling out the lunch she'd packed for them.

"Then you'd be dealing with hikers and campers traipsing through your backyard." He took the sandwich and napkin she handed him. "Did you grow up in Rosewood?"

"No, but the town I grew up in was about the same size. Saddle Brook, Oklahoma, is about an hour and a half from here. Mark and I met at college. We were both business majors, but he was a year ahead of me. He proposed to me right after my graduation, and the rest, as they say, is history." After making sure they had everything they needed, she unwrapped her sandwich. "What about you? Small town, big city?"

"Somewhere in between. White Plains is about thirty minutes north of New York City and has a population of around sixty thousand. My foster father was a police sergeant there, and his wife was a teacher before they started fostering kids. They didn't have any of their own and felt with their backgrounds they'd be perfect foster parents . . . and they were."

Swallowing a bite of her sandwich, Sage washed it down with some water. "You mentioned you were with them in your teens. What about before that? Did you know your biological parents?"

Adam nodded. "Sort of. I never knew my father, and I was eight when the state took me away from my mother due to abuse and neglect. Apparently, she left town after that, and I never saw her again."

Her eyes widened in horror. "Oh, my God. Adam, I'm so sorry. That must've been awful." Her heart clenched for the young boy he'd been and what he'd gone through. "You don't have to talk about this if you don't want."

"It's all right." He shrugged. "From what I remember, I was better off after she left. I had no other known relatives —my mother was an only child, and her parents died before I was born. I never really knew anything about them other than I was named after my grandfather. After social services stepped in, I was bounced around from one foster home to another, never finding one where I felt I fit in. Finally, when I was fourteen and had just gotten kicked out of another home for fighting, I was placed with Harry and Barbara. It took a little while, but with their guidance and love, I was able to start dealing with all my issues of abandonment and lack of self-worth. They got me and my foster brother, Shane, involved in sports, camping, volunteering to help others . . . all sorts of stuff, instead of letting us just sit idly wasting away."

"They sound like a great couple." She could hear the love and respect he had for them in his voice.

"They were. They're both gone now, but it's because of them I didn't end up on the streets as a drug addict or worse."

Sage shuddered, thinking about all the things that did and could've happened to Adam growing up. "How did you find your way to the Brotherhood?"

She couldn't picture him as a friar. All she'd been able to conjure up in her mind was the portly Friar Tuck character from *Robin Hood* fame. And Adam was far from "portly."

"An old friend of Harry's was a friar and would come for

dinner every few Sundays to visit. Harry and Barbara were also members of his congregation. Shane and I had the option of volunteering for four hours every Sunday at a soup kitchen or going to church, which was only an hour." He smirked. "You can guess which one we picked. Anyway, in my senior year of high school, I started volunteering with Brother Leo's youth group. It was there that I finally felt I'd found my direction in life.

"At first, I thought it was just leading me into social work, psychology, or some field like that, where I could help people, but during my first year of college, I realized it was something more. I talked to Brother Leo about it, and as you said before, the rest is history. Once I was assigned to a church, I continued my involvement with the kids and teens. Harry had gotten Shane and me into boxing, wrestling, and martial arts to show us we could defend ourselves yet have the discipline not to start fights, to begin with. So, I passed that on to the next generation."

She was in awe of this man who'd overcome so much and ended up taking a road most men these days would never give a single glance. "Do you miss it?"

Adam tilted his head to the side and wiped his mouth with his napkin. "In the beginning, I did, but I also was too busy trying to survive prison. Then I realized I didn't have to be in the Brotherhood in order to guide and help others. I can do that anywhere . . . even from a six-by-eight cell."

"You're amazing."

Oh. My. God. Did I just say that aloud and breathlessly?

From the pink tinge in his cheeks, it was obvious she had. "I mean, I've never met anyone like you. So many people would've let what happened to them beat them down, but you didn't." It was clear he was a little embarrassed about her praise. Picking up the remains of their meal, she stuffed it all back into the saddlebag to be thrown in the garbage later. "Ready to head back? I want to check on the foal and make sure she's nursing properly."

He stood and held out his hand, which she took and allowed him to help her up. "Lead on, boss. Just no racing back. I'm going to be sore enough as it is."

They were almost back to the barn when Sage sensed something was wrong. Something . . . she inhaled and smelled . . . smoke? Her gaze searched frantically, and when she found the source, her stomach dropped. "Oh, my God! The barn is on fire!"

Not waiting for Adam, she dug her heels into Topaz's flanks and took off at a full gallop. Diamond Lil and her filly, the other two nursing mares with their thirteen-day-old offspring, and one of the pregnant mares were still inside, while the others had been placed in a one-acre enclosure this morning.

Pulling up on the reins, she jumped off the horse before it had come to a complete halt and ran into the barn. Flames were shooting along the back wall near the tack room and quickly spreading. The horses panicked in their locked stalls, and she worked fast to unlatch the doors and swing them open. The smoke was getting thick, and her eyes stung as her lungs struggled for air. The first two mares, with their foals following, bolted from their stalls, heading for the exit. Turning to the next stall, Sage struggled to find the latch as the smoke limited her sight.

"Sage! Where are you?" She barely heard him over the roar of the fire, the crackling of wood, and the shrieking horses. Half the barn was engulfed, but it wouldn't take long before the entire thing fell down around her.

"Adam! Help me get the horses! Get Diamond Lil and the baby!" Her fingers found the latch, and she threw the door open, almost getting run over as a pregnant Baby Ruth burst from the stall. Her chest tightened with the lack of oxygen, and Sage coughed violently as she tried to see through the blinding smoke. "Adam!"

"I've got them! Go! Get out!"

Praying he was right behind her, she ran for the door and gulped for fresh air. Sirens sounded in the distance. Someone must have seen the smoke and called 9-1-1.

Spinning around, she jumped out of the way when Diamond Lil emerged from the smoke at full speed, her eyes wide with terror. Seconds later, Adam stumbled out carrying the young foal. They had all made it . . . thank God.

Chapter Six

Evan's truck pulled up the drive as the volunteer firefighters were putting away the last of the hoses. The barn was a total loss, but they'd kept the flames from spreading to Adam's cottage and the surrounding area. Evan, Maddie, and Jenna hurried over to Adam and Sage, fear and worry written on their faces.

"Mommy!"

Sage bent at the waist as her frightened daughter leaped into her arms, and she hugged her tight. "It's okay, sweetheart. No one was hurt, and the horses are all safe."

"Even Ruby Tuethday," Jenna sniffled.

"Even Ruby. Adam saved her."

The little girl looked at him with big, watery eyes. "You did?" When he nodded, she added, "Thank you, Adam."

He ruffled her blonde hair. "You're welcome, Little Bird. Why don't you and Maddie go check on all of them in the front pen?"

When the two of them were out of earshot, Adam turned to Evan. "It was no accident."

"What?" The older man was as stunned as Adam and Sage had been when the fire chief had told them it looked as if an accelerant had been sprayed on the back wall. The chief also pointed out that there seemed to be several points of origin, indicating the fire started in multiple spots. The man was currently filling in the sheriff, who'd pulled up moments before.

"Unfortunately, we didn't see anybody. It was only by a stroke of luck that we were back in time to save the horses." Adam stared at Sage. She'd been awfully quiet after the chief had hit them with the news. It was obvious to him she was trying to fight back tears and remain strong in front of everyone, but this was one more thing she didn't need in her life. Grabbing Evan's elbow, Adam pulled him out of her hearing range as she stood silently, facing the gutted-out structure. "Do they do things like good old-fashioned barn raisings around here anymore, or is that a thing of the past?"

The older man wiped his brow and grinned. "We sure do, son. I'll get on the horn and have a posse here first thing in the morning. We'll have the rest of this knocked down and cleared out in no time." He scratched his chin. "We may have to put the lumber on credit, though. I'll have to check with Sage about that. I don't think the barn was covered under her insurance, just the horses."

"You let me worry about that." Adam had a few things up his sleeve that he didn't want to advertise. He'd contact Shane later to set things in motion. "You just start on those phone calls and get as many people as you can to help. And why don't you ask Maddie to order pizza or something simple tonight."

"Good idea."

After Evan left to get things underway, Adam strode over to where Sage was now talking to the sheriff. The gray-haired man eyed him warily as he approached. Sage halted whatever she'd been saying to introduce the two men. "Adam, this is Sheriff Pete Cosgrove. Sheriff, this my new ranch hand, Adam Westfield."

The man hesitated before shaking Adam's outstretched hand. His tone of voice was dry and seemingly unimpressed. "So I've heard."

Adam raised an eyebrow. "Really? Guess word travels fast in small towns like Rosewood."

"Uh-huh. I make it a practice to find out what I can about strangers who suddenly take up residence in my town. Imagine my surprise when I learned Ms. Hammond hired an ex-con. Where were you when the fire started, Mr. Westfield?"

Beside him, Sage gasped. "Who the hell did you hear that from? I swear this town has more gossips than a zebra has fucking stripes—it pisses me off." She put one hand on her hip and shook a finger at the uniformed man. "You have no right to accuse Adam of anything because of his past, Sheriff. He was with *me*, riding the horses along the ridge. And—"

Placing a steady hand on her shoulder, Adam interrupted, "It's okay, Sage. Sheriff, if you have any questions about my past, then ask them. But as for the fire, I think you might take your questions about that up the road."

The man's bushy eyebrows came together as he frowned. "What's that supposed to mean?"

"It means that Bart Sherman has been trying to buy this land for the past several years. Sage turned him down again the other day, and he didn't seem happy about it. Makes me wonder what a man would resort to if he didn't get what he wanted."

"Now, wait a minute. Bart Sherman is a respected member of the community—"

"And I'm just an ex-con who served my time." He still wasn't used to some people's reaction when they found out he'd been in prison, but there was nothing he could do about it. They were entitled to their opinions, and there was little he could do to change someone's mind if they were already convinced he was an evil person. "Now, if you don't have any more questions for Ms. Hammond or myself, then excuse us. We have a lot of cleaning up to do."

Tightening his hand on Sage's shoulder, he steered her back toward the house.

"Adam, I'm so sorry. He had no right to accuse you."

He leaned against the railing post next to the porch steps and crossed his arms. "It's not your fault, and he's just doing his job."

"It's still not right."

Grinning, he brushed his thumb across her cheek, which was covered in soot. "Anyone ever tell you that you're adorable when you pout?" Not waiting for an answer, he continued, "Listen. Why don't you go shower? I'll check on the horses and make sure they have enough water. They can stay there for the night, right? And get by on the grass until we can replace the feed in the morning?"

She sighed, then nodded. "Yeah, they should be fine. Benji will alert us if anything is wrong. Thanks for helping me save the horses."

"No thanks necessary. I'm just glad we made it in time."

A few hours later, after the lights in the main house were turned off, Adam was leaning on the fence watching the horses settle in for the night. Holding his cell phone to his ear, he gave Shane the number to the local lumber yard that Evan had supplied him with. Their foster parents had named their two longtime charges as benefactors in their will. Shane was the executor and kept Adam's money in a separate account. It had been originally set up that way because it was well known that the medical insurance coverage the church had for its priests and friars was lacking in long-term care. This way, if anything happened to Adam, Shane could get him the best treatment and doctors available. He never thought he would need it for anything else. Now he was glad he had access to it.

"So, besides the fire, how are things in Rosewood, Oklahoma?" Shane asked.

He took a deep breath and blurted, "I kissed her."

"What? Who?" Shane sounded as shocked as Adam felt.

"I kissed Sage."

There was an extended pause on the other end of the line. "And?"

Adam chuckled, taking a moment to enjoy drawing out the suspense he knew was killing the other man. "And what?"

"Come on, Adam," Shane huffed. "This isn't the eighteenth century, and despite being a modern-day friar, it's not the first time you've kissed a member of the opposite sex. Wait. That's all it was, right? A kiss? Or more?"

"Just a kiss." But, damn, how he'd wanted more.

There was an even longer pause this time before Shane spoke again. "You're not going to ask me for pointers here, are you? I mean, I love you, bro, but that would be just too weird."

He rolled his eyes. "Don't worry. I'm not going there with you. I think I can remember the basics."

"Well, just remember to use protection."

"Yes, Harry." Adam loved to tease Shane when he started sounding like their foster father.

"Shit. The baby's crying. I've got to get her before she wakes up Nicole—she was exhausted going to bed earlier. I'll take care of that stuff first thing in the morning. Love ya, bro."

"Love you, too. Kiss my pretty niece for me and the rest of the family too."

Shane was already making cooing noises to little Melanie before he disconnected the call, and Adam smiled. His brother had offered to let him stay with them when he'd first gotten out of prison, but Adam couldn't do that to them. Shane and Nicole had two boys, ages four and six, and Melanie had arrived two months before Adam's release from prison. He'd only stayed with them for two nights before hitting the road, not wanting to intrude on them any more than necessary.

Strolling back to his cottage, his mind kept flipping between the fire in the barn and the one he felt in his gut and other places whenever he thought about kissing Sage. And how much he wanted to do it again.

———— ❤ ————

SAGE WOKE TO THE SOUNDS OF BANGING, MEN'S VOICES, AND THE beeping of a vehicle being backed up. Glancing at the clock, she was shocked to see it was ten minutes to nine. She never slept that late. Throwing the covers off, she stood and hurried to the window. What she saw was controlled chaos, and she tried to wrap her still-slumbering brain around what was going on in her backyard. Over two dozen men were clearing out the remains of the barn and placing them in huge dumpsters. A backhoe was being used for the larger pieces. Those not involved in the clean-up were on the far side of the wreckage, hammering together pieces of lumber into what she assumed was the back wall of her new barn. "Holy crap!"

Grabbing clothes to change into, she quickly took care of things in the bathroom and rushed out to the kitchen, where she found Maddie, Ashley, and two other women, Sarah Pickler and Jess Donahue, cooking up a storm.

Ashley spotted her first. "Well, it's about time you joined us. How could you sleep with all this racket? Oh, and don't worry about the kids. Matthew is at my place with Toby. Chris's mother is watching them. And Jenna is over at Cara Albertson's for the day. She said to call her later and let her know if you want Jenna to sleep over there."

Her friend shoved a fresh mug of coffee in Sage's hand as she eyed all the food the others were preparing to take out to the workers. "What's going on?"

Maddie chuckled. "A good, old-fashioned barn raising is what's going on. Adam and Evan got the ball rolling last night, and everyone started showing up at the crack of dawn."

Tears filled her eyes. This was one of the reasons she did love living in a small town. Despite everyone knowing everyone else's business, they would all pull together to help each other out in times of need. She'd lain in bed last night, unable to fall asleep immediately even though she'd been exhausted, trying to figure out where she would get the extra money to rebuild the barn. Speaking of which . . . "Where did the lumber come from?"

Grinning, Maddie pointed toward the backdoor. "Why

71

don't you go outside and ask Adam? I believe that was all his doing."

Adam? He'd arranged it? How? From what she'd seen from her window, there was a small fortune in materials out there. "Thanks. And thank you all for being here." Her voice cracked. "It—it means a lot to me."

After each woman hugged her and brushed off her gratitude as not being necessary, Sage took her coffee and headed out back. From the porch, she took in all the activity going on. To her right, the llamas and sheep were grazing at the far side of their large, enclosed pasture. The loud banging was probably the reason for that. The first person she spotted was Reverend Stevens. The man was in his fifties and had no trouble helping with hard labor. He was usually the first one to volunteer when someone needed assistance.

"Morning, Sage."

"Good morning, Reverend. Thank you so much for coming out to help." She gestured with her hand to the activity buzzing around them. "You don't know how much this means to me."

He stepped out of the way as two other men hauled a charred post that once held up the barn over to the dumpster. "The congregation always helps out when someone needs us. You should know that by now since you've been on the other side several times when others needed help."

It was true, she'd been to several barn raisings and fundraisers over the years, but it was still humbling to be on the receiving end. Glancing up from his hammering, Ashley's husband, Chris, gave Sage a wave and a grin before returning to his carpentry. Chris and Mark had been best friends, and she knew he still felt the tragic loss as much as she did.

Behind her, the old dinner bell on the porch started clanging, and she turned to see Maddie pulling on the string as the other women carried all the food out to the folding tables they'd set up. "Come and get it while it's hot, gentlemen. Breakfast is ready."

The men finished what they were currently doing and all ambled over for the mini-feast of coffee, eggs, bacon, home fries, grits, pancakes, and more. Sage thanked everyone as they walked past her. Adam was the last one to reach her, and without a second thought, she stepped forward and hugged him.

He hesitated a moment before wrapping his arms around her. "What's this for?"

"For taking care of all this for me. It's unbelievable." Not letting him go, she pulled back to see his face. "But, tell me one thing. Where did the lumber come from? I don't know where I'll get the money to pay for it before the foals are sold."

"Don't worry about it. I have an inheritance from Harry and Barbara that Shane manages for me. Consider it a gift for taking a chance and hiring me."

Stunned, she shook her head. "Adam, I can't ask you to pay for it. It's too expensive. I'll repay you when I sell the horses."

"Absolutely not." He took her hands in his, his eyes and voice pleading with her. "Please, Sage." When she started to shake her head again, he clutched her hands tighter. "Do you remember me telling you I found new ways to help people outside of the Brotherhood? Well, this is one of them. I like to think I'm investing in Jenna and Matthew's futures. Please, let me do this for them . . . and you."

She didn't know what to say, so instead, she pulled him close, went up on her toes, and pressed her lips to his.

Fireworks went off in her mind when he kissed her right back, molding his mouth to hers. Tentatively, his tongue eased out and traced the seam of her lips. Opening them, she let her tongue duel with his. She completely forgot where they were and who else was there until she heard a chorus of catcalls and whistles. Ending the kiss, she gazed into his eyes, which were filled with a combination of lust and amusement. "Thank you."

He cleared his throat. "You're very welcome. Come on. Let's go eat before it's all gone."

Taking a step back, he took her hand and led her to the porch. She tried to hide her embarrassment, but Reverend Stevens caught her eye and gave her a wink. It was obvious he approved—however, Ashley didn't look very happy with what just occurred, if her frown was any indication.

After breakfast, Seth Chapman and his oldest boy, Danny, arrived along with two other men. The three pickup trucks they came in carried bales of new hay along with feed and supplements for the horses, llamas, sheep, and chickens, all of which had been lost in the fire with the spare tackle. At least the two saddles and bridles which had been on Othello and Topaz were saved—everything else she could borrow from friends or buy second-hand.

Sage was helping clear up the last of the breakfast platters when Seth strode up to her and, as usual, got a little too close for her comfort. "Hey, darlin'. So sorry to hear about this. The fire chief is saying it was arson. Who'd you piss off?"

Taking a step back, she crossed her arms and glared at him. "Why do you assume I pissed someone off, Seth? It could have been any number of reasons why someone would've set fire to my barn. Maybe it was some crazed lunatic."

The man shrugged and smirked. "Well, if you had a man around, maybe it would scare off whoever was responsible. I keep telling you, I'm available for the job."

She was about to say something snarky when the screen door swung open, and Adam stepped out carrying two bags of garbage for the dumpsters. *Perfect timing.*

Grabbing his arm before he got past them, Sage pulled him closer, ignoring his startled expression. "Actually, Seth, I already have a man around. This is Adam Westfield. Adam, this is Seth Chapman. Adam is my new ranch hand . . . and he's also my new boyfriend."

One of the garbage bags fell to the ground with a thump and some glass clinking. She saw she'd caught Adam off guard, but Seth seemed oblivious that anything was amiss. His jaw had dropped as he stared at her before his eyes shifted to Adam, who'd recovered and was now holding out his hand. "Nice to meet you, Seth. Thanks for coming to help out."

Seth appeared reluctant but took the proffered hand and shook it once before releasing it. Sage could see a tick in his temple, and she fought back the giggle. Hopefully, she'd found a way to prevent further pick-up lines from him.

"Not from around here, are you Westfield?" The man looked ready to spit nails.

Adam smiled knowingly and put his arm around her shoulder, tucking her against his side. For a former celibate friar, the man caught on quickly. "As Sage keeps telling me, my New York accent gives me away every time. Isn't that right, honey?"

Resisting the urge to roll her eyes, Sage tried to send him a telepathic message, thanking him for playing along but not to lay it on too thick. "Yes, I do keep telling you that, and maybe now you'll believe me . . . sweetie."

One of the men unloading the bales of hay from the trucks next to Adam's cottage whistled loudly, and they all turned to see him staring at them. "Hey, Seth! You going to work or stand there and yap while we take care of everything . . . again."

"Fuck you, Charlie . . . oh, sorry, Reverend." At least the man blushed in remorse for his language when he spotted the holy man coming up the steps. "I'm coming."

The jerk brushed past Reverend Stevens, who approached Sage with an ash-covered metal box. "We found this back where the tack room was."

Stunned, she took it from him. "Oh, my . . ." Cracking open the lid, she stared in awe, and tears welled up in her eyes. She lifted her gaze to Adam and tried to speak, but nothing came out.

He pulled a bandanna from the back pocket of his jeans and held it out to her. "What is it, Sage?"

Swallowing hard, she wiped her eyes with the red and white cloth before placing the box on one of the breakfast tables. Slowly, she shifted through the contents. "It's stuff Mark began saving after he and I started dating in college. He kept everything. I forgot all about it and haven't seen this stuff since before Matthew was born. Mark must've kept it in his workbench. Letters I wrote him. Movie and concert ticket stubs." She pulled out a strip of four photos and showed it to him. "This was from our second date. There was a photo booth at a carnival."

"You haven't changed much over the years."

She snorted. "Thanks, but compared to now, I look like I was fifteen in that photo." Her hair had been longer then, and now she still carried around some of the baby weight she'd never lost after Jenna was born. She looked at the

Reverend. "Thank you so much for finding this and not assuming it was trash."

He patted her hand. "The Lord works in mysterious ways."

As the man returned to help with the rest of the clean-up, Sage put everything back in the box and shut it. "I'll look through this later," she told Adam. "For now, I'll put it in my room. I'll be right back."

"Take your time. I have garbage to dispose of . . . honey."

She grinned as he walked away, chuckling. "Thank you, sweetie."

Six hours later, the remnants of the fire had been hauled away, and the frame of the new barn was completed. The floor had been laid, and stalls had been roped off while tarps were placed in what would be the loft to make a temporary shelter for the horses. The men finished storing the tools in their trucks and vowed to return tomorrow to finish the job.

After cleaning up, Sage sent Maddie and Evan back to their cabin with plates of leftover food from lunch. A few more women had shown up a little before 1:00 p.m. with trays of food—enough to feed a small army. Despite their big breakfasts, the men had worked up an appetite and had been enthusiastic about filling their stomachs once more. But there'd been plenty of food left over, and Maddie had sent dinner home with whoever had wanted it.

Her hair still wet from a fast shower, Sage popped one plate and then another into the microwave, reheating meals, consisting of a little taste of everything, for Adam and herself. The timer dinged at the same time the screen door opened, and he walked in, fresh from his own shower.

He'd also shaved again, which made her crave to stroke the baby-soft skin before his whiskers returned.

Taking the plates from her, he carried them into the dining room while she grabbed two bottles of beer from the fridge. She'd found out, even as a friar, he'd enjoyed the occasional brew. Following him, she stopped short, surprised by his seat choice. Instead of sitting at the opposite end of the table from Sage, where he normally sat, he'd set his plate down where Jenna usually sat.

Waiting for her to sit, he raised an eyebrow. "Problem? I'll sit at the other end if you want."

Smiling, she shook her head and set the beer bottles on the table. "Don't you dare move. Let me just get the glasses I put in the freezer earlier."

When she returned, he held out her chair for her to sit. Inwardly, she felt warm fuzzies throughout her body. It was such a simple act of being a gentleman, but it made her feel special and pampered. "Thank you."

"You're welcome." Sitting, he took hold of her hand and said grace. "Thank you, Lord, for this food we are about to eat. For our family and friends. And for the community that pulled together to help us in our time of need. Bless them all. Amen."

"Amen."

They both dug into their food. Sage hadn't realized how hungry she was until a bite of baked ziti hit her taste buds. "*Mmm.* I love Ashley's tomato sauce. Her lasagna has won blue ribbons at the July Fourth county fair more times than it's lost. Her only real competition is Hilde, who owns the diner in town."

"If it's as good as her ziti, then I'm sure it's a winner." Adam took another bite, then swallowed. "Now I'm going to have to try Hilde's sauce and judge for myself. But this ranks right up there with my foster mother's. She was a hell of a cook." He picked up his beer. "What about you? What food do you enter in the county fair?"

An unladylike snort escaped her. "I'm not allowed to enter anything. No one wants to risk food poisoning. Thank goodness for Maddie, otherwise, we'd live on sandwiches and frozen dinners."

Adam grinned as he cut a piece of ham. "You can't be that bad."

"You have no idea. If it's not microwaveable or cold, then it's not on my menu unless someone else makes it. But Maddie will be entering a few pies and her five-alarm chili at the fair."

"I'll have to watch her make her chili. It was another of Barbara's best meals."

After finishing their meal, they made fast work of cleaning the dishes and putting away the leftovers. Sage poured them both a cup of coffee she'd brewed while heating up their dinner, and they brought them out to the front porch. She sat on the two-person wooden swing and indicated for him to join her.

They sat in silence as Adam used his foot to swing them gently back and forth. This was one of Sage's favorite things to do after everyone else had gone to sleep for the night. She could sit here, remember the good times with Mark, and cry over her loss without her children being the wiser. Not that she always ended up in tears, but if she did, she didn't have to worry about Matthew and Jenna seeing her upset.

The more she spent time with Adam, the more she liked him. She couldn't imagine what it'd been like for him in prison. While her uncle had been in and out of the local jail in her hometown due to his excessive drinking, she'd never known anyone who'd been locked up for more than a day or two. "May I ask you something?"

Adam kept the swing moving. "Sure."

Sage shifted her hips to face him a little better. She hoped he wouldn't think she was judging him. "Why . . . *um* . . . from what Shane told me, if you had gone to trial, you would have been found innocent. Why did you plead guilty?"

Chapter Seven

Adam took a deep breath and let it out slowly. How could he explain this so she would understand what he'd felt back then? What he still felt deep down in his soul? "I . . . uh . . . well, for starters, I didn't want the boy to have to testify. He was twelve at the time—old enough to be very embarrassed about telling a roomful of adults what had been done to him. And it wouldn't be once. He'd have to testify twice—for the grand jury and then, if they handed down an indictment, a trial jury. I couldn't do that to him—it was bad enough he would be reliving it in therapy for years with only one psychiatrist in the room."

He leaned over and placed his now cold coffee on the wooden floor next to the swing. "Then I was dealing with my own guilt of not realizing what Brother Andre had been up to for years. The crime scene techs found evidence in his bedroom that led them to at least fifteen other young boys he'd molested—and that was over the eight years he was with us in New York. He'd come from another monastery in California, so who knows how many kids he'd abused." His shoulders sagged with regret. "And finally . . . I took a life . . . one that wasn't mine to take."

Sage shook her head, and her eyes narrowed. "But Shane said it was an accident—when you stopped him, he fell and hit his head. How is that your fault?"

Halting the swing, Adam stood suddenly and stepped toward the railing before turning around and leaning against it. Staring at her, his expression pleaded with her to understand as he tried to explain what'd happened after his initial confusion at what he'd walked in on had been replaced by an anger he'd never known existed in him.

"Shane wasn't there." He ran a hand down his face, trying to control his emotions. "I-I saw red, and all the martial arts and discipline training Harry had put me and Shane through went out the window. I lost all control—all of it. In a rage, I threw Andre across the room, and when he came after me, I put everything I had into a punch. He wasn't an experienced fighter and was shorter and weighed less than me. It—it wouldn't have taken much to hold him down and wait for the police. But that's not what I did, Sage. I hit him—hard. When he went down, his head cracked against the corner of a wooden chest."

Adam paused and swallowed hard. This was the first time he'd described what'd happened in detail to anyone since the police interrogation. Shane had tried to tell him to shut up and wait for a lawyer, but Adam hadn't been able to stop the confession from pouring out of him. Now, gazing into Sage's eyes, he told her something he'd never told anyone—not even his brother. "So help me, God, if he'd gotten up, I would have hit him again and again, Sage. Either way, I honestly believe the result would have been the same. And in my mind . . . my heart . . . and my soul, that made me a murderer."

Adam hadn't realized fat tears were rolling down his face until Sage stood and brushed them away with her fingers. She pulled him into her arms and held him as he silently cried on her shoulder. His heart was filled with anguish as she rubbed his back with her flat palms and spoke softly to him.

"*Shh.* Adam, it's okay. You didn't do it on purpose. Most people I've met in life would have reacted the same way, myself included. It just means you're not perfect . . . it means you're human. And isn't that why Jesus died on that cross? Because all of us are human."

In too much emotional pain to be embarrassed, Adam wrapped his arms around Sage's waist and held her tightly. Resting his head on her shoulder, he wasn't sure how long they stood there, but as his tears began to wane, he realized he felt lighter than he had in years. Somehow, someway, this beautiful woman was helping him purge his sins.

Taking a deep, shuddering breath, he lifted his head, and their gazes met. All he saw in her eyes was understanding, compassion, and . . . forgiveness—something he hadn't sought from her, but she gave him willingly.

Her expression softened, and she was no longer staring into his eyes but, instead, at his mouth. Bending, he brushed his lips against hers and could swear she melted in his arms, so he did it again . . . and again. Each time, the contact was deeper, harder, and more mesmerizing.

Adam took her bottom lip between his and flicked his tongue over the plump flesh. Sage's arms slid up his shoulders and around his neck, pulling him closer. Her mouth opened, inviting him in to taste her . . . it was an invitation he couldn't refuse.

His tongue delved inside, and suddenly, the embarrassment he'd lacked earlier arose. Was he doing it right? Was she enjoying it, or did she think he was a lousy kisser? *Jeez*, a thirty-eight-year-old man shouldn't have these insecurities, he thought wryly.

A sensual moan escaped Sage, and he felt it all the way to his toes. Her body rubbed against his like a seductive kitten, and his cock grew harder. Turning, he positioned her between the railing and his body, trapping her in place. His mouth left hers and peppered her jaw and neck with kisses until he reached her ear, which he licked and nuzzled. She wore no perfume, but her citrus shampoo and body wash, mixed with her own unique scent, was driving him crazy.

He craved her more than he'd ever craved anything else in his life. It went beyond the wants and needs of any heterosexual male in an intimate setting with a woman. It was as if she'd been born to be the only woman for him. Was Sage his chance to be whole again? His fate? His soulmate?

Around the back of the house, Benji barked at something—probably a rabbit—and just like that, the spell between the couple was broken. They both stiffened at the same time as if realizing things would've gone much further if the dog hadn't barked some sense back into them.

Adam sighed, then whispered, "As much as I'd like to continue, I think we should stop. It's been a long day, and tomorrow will be even longer. We both need to get some sleep before the troops return at eight."

When she pulled back, he saw lust mixed with a bit of disappointment written all over her face. And that wouldn't do. "Trust me when I say letting you go to bed alone is the last thing I want to do, but we agreed to take this slow. This is all new for me, Sage. I don't want to screw it up . . ." He cupped her jawline and looked her straight in the eye. "Not with you."

Sage bit her lower lip and nodded with obvious reluctance. "You're right . . . we did say we'd take this slow. You're also right that we need to get some sleep, but I just want to go on the record as saying letting you go to bed alone is the last thing I want to do too."

She placed a kiss on his lips . . . a very chaste kiss. "I'm sorry I asked about—"

Squeezing his hands around her waist, he cut her off with a shake of his head. "I'm not. That was something I needed to get off my chest for a very long time. I should be thanking you. That's the first time I'd told anyone everything . . . how I felt at the time and how I've felt ever since. And that includes Shane. So, please, don't say you're sorry because I'm not."

"Well, then, instead of being sorry . . ." A slow, sexy grin spread across Sage's face. ". . . I'll be grateful. For someone who hasn't kissed a woman in almost twenty years, you're not half bad."

Adam let out a hearty laugh and put a southern twang into his voice. "Why, thank you, ma'am . . . I think. I look forward to practicing some more." He took a step back because if he didn't, neither one of them would get the sleep they needed tonight. Tilting his head toward the front door, he said, "Go on to bed. I'll do a quick check on the horses before turning in. I'll see you in the morning."

As Sage sashayed her way into the house, he groaned and shifted his hips. After she disappeared, his gaze went to the star-filled heavens. "You do know that woman could tempt the saints, don't you?"

God didn't answer him . . . but someday, in His own way, He would.

———— ❤ ————

CARRYING TWO LARGE BOWLS FILLED WITH MACARONI AND POTATO salad, Sage followed Ashley out to the back porch, where they were once again setting up to feed the troops. The new barn was almost complete, thanks to the two dozen people who'd been working hard on it for the past two days. Hammers pounded, and nail guns banged with every new two-by-four, sheet of plywood, and roof shingle that went up. She noticed several men were starting to clean up their work areas and realized the barn would be complete by the end of the day.

Without conscious effort, Sage's gaze found Adam easily among the men. In a snug, white T-shirt, faded jeans, and his work boots, he was easy on the eyes, more so than any other she'd seen since Mark. Her thoughts went back to the night before, and she remembered how it felt to be in his arms, comforting him . . . kissing him. She felt a stirring in her womb.

"Are you going to put down the salads or stand there drooling over him all day?"

There was no mistaking the disapproval in Ashley's voice. Placing the bowls on the table, Sage turned to her best friend and tried to feign indifference. "I'm not drooling over anyone. I was just . . . just looking to see how much more work needed to be done. I can't believe they got the barn back up that fast."

"Uh-huh." Ashley crossed her arms and leaned a hip against the food-laden table, concern written on her face. "Look, I know it's not any of my business, but I'm worried about you, Sage. I mean, what do you really know about Adam? Okay, so he's a hard worker, and he bought the lumber for you—I'm not saying that wasn't really nice of him—but I can't help but think he's trying to buy his way into your bed. Everyone can see how you're falling for him. What are you going to do when he decides to move on again? He told you he's been moving from town to town, doing odd jobs since he got out of prison. What makes you think he's going to stay here? And don't get me started on the prison thing."

Apparently not heeding her own advice, Ashley started in on it. "Think about Matthew and Jenna. If he does stick around, do you really want an ex-con influencing your children? And what if he doesn't stay? It'll break their hearts if you've let them get close to him. They already lost Mark—do you want them to get attached and then lose Adam too?"

Several times during the other woman's speech, Sage had opened her mouth to respond, but Ashley hadn't let her get a word in. Now, though, she was thinking hard about what her best friend had pointed out. Not about Adam buying his way into her bed—Sage knew much more about Adam than her friend did, and it wasn't her place to fill Ashley in about everything. But what if Jenna and Matthew did get too attached to Adam, and then he packed up and left?

What if I get too attached and he leaves?

He hadn't mentioned anything about staying long-term. And Ashley was right, he had told her he'd been wandering around the states, taking odd jobs when he needed to.

But what about the savings he'd tapped into to purchase the lumber supplies? That hadn't been cheap. *So why did he even need to find work wherever he went?*

Suddenly, Sage was so confused. She'd let her sexual awareness of the man rule her body, but what she needed to do was listen to her brain instead. Ashley was right—she needed to do what was best for her and the children. There were other men—stable men with ties to the community—who'd asked her out over the past year, and she'd turned them all down. Maybe the next time one of them asked her out, she'd accept.

The sound of cheering brought her out of her musing. Ashley was smiling at her again. "They're all done. Let's go check out your new barn."

By the time it was dark and everyone had left, Sage had herself convinced her best friend was right. She needed to keep Adam at a distance, protecting her heart and her children. Ashley had even told her that Frank Browning had been asking about her lately, and she would set the two up on a date if Sage were interested. The local high school history teacher was a widower with two kids. Ashley had chuckled and said they could be the *Brady Bunch* minus two.

After ensuring the front and rear doors were locked, Sage flipped off the kitchen light and strode quietly down the hall toward her bedroom. As she neared Jenna's closed door, she stopped short—her little girl was crying! Opening the door, her eyes went wide with alarm. Jenna was lying in bed, hugging the stuffing out of her teddy bear, with tears rolling down her face.

Sage hurried over and placed her hand on Jenna's forehead, checking for a fever and not finding her hot. Sitting on the bed, she pulled her sobbing daughter into her lap, wrapped her arms around her, and rocked back and forth. "Sweetheart, what's wrong? *Shh.* It's okay—tell Mommy what's wrong."

That just made Jenna cry harder.

"Are you hurt or sick?"

Her daughter shook her head, her small body racked with shuddering sobs and hiccups.

"Then what is it, sweetie?"

"Th-the . . . the d-d . . . dancth."

Suddenly, Sage understood, and her heart sank. With the barn fire and all the activity over the past two days, she'd forgotten all about the father/daughter dance this Saturday at the church hall. It was an annual event for the Brownies and Girl Scouts. This was the first time since Mark's death something like this had come up for Jenna. She'd joined the local Brownie troop a month after last year's dance. When Sage had seen it on this year's schedule, she'd planned to do something fun for Jenna so she wouldn't feel left out. Last month, Evan had offered to take her until Maddie had reminded him that this weekend was their niece's wedding. The young woman was also Maddie's goddaughter, so they had to go.

Continuing to rock Jenna, Sage murmured that it would be all right until the little girl's body stilled with exhaustion. She waited a few minutes to make sure Jenna was indeed down for the count, then laid her on the bed and pulled the covers over her limp body. Taking a deep breath, Sage stood and tiptoed out of the room, wiping away her own tears as she closed the door.

Chapter Eight

Adam put a handful of wildflowers into a mason jar filled with water and scanned the living room of his cabin, making sure all was in order. Everything was perfect. He actually had butterflies in his stomach as he glanced at his watch—*two more minutes*. The last time he'd asked a female out was in his first year of college, and he hoped he wouldn't screw it up. Tonight would be special, and he hoped she thought so too.

Dragging a hand down his newly shaved face, he checked the mirror by the front door and adjusted the tie he'd borrowed from Evan. Although he wore a clean pair of jeans, the button-down dress shirt he wore to church was doing double duty this week. He'd run a comb through his wet hair and slicked it back.

Footsteps outside the front door told him the time had come seconds before there was a light knock on the wood. Taking a deep breath, he turned and pulled the door knob. A smile spread across his face at the pretty sight before him, and he had to bite his lip to keep from laughing when Matthew and Sage both gave him a thumbs-up. Jenna was standing on the other side of the threshold, wearing a pink and white dress, white patent leather shoes, a pink ribbon in her hair, and a blue bandanna covering her eyes. Matthew's hands were on her shoulders as he stood behind her and guided her. She had no idea where she was going and why.

Waving them forward, Adam took a few steps back as Matthew steered his sister into the room. Adam then knelt on the floor in front of her and picked up the sign he'd made that afternoon after clearing everything with Sage earlier. This coming weekend was a Brownies' and Girl Scouts' father/daughter dance, and Jenna had been crying because she didn't have Mark to take her. He'd overheard Sage and Maddie discussing the little girl's sorrow after breakfast that morning.

When Adam had first approached Sage with the offer to take her, she'd originally said no. Not because she didn't want Adam taking Mark's place in her daughter's life, but because she was afraid Jenna was getting too attached to Adam. She didn't want the little girl to go through the loss of another father figure when he eventually left town. But an hour later, she'd come out to the barn to find him and said she'd changed her mind. It would mean a lot to the little girl to go to the dance with him, and Jenna's happiness was all that mattered now.

Adam wished he'd had the courage to say he wasn't going anywhere, that he wanted to stay here with Sage and her children, but he'd been too chicken. He had no idea where he stood with Sage—how she truly felt about him. From what he understood, she hadn't been involved with any man since Mark's death. Adam might just be a stepping stone for her to return to the dating world. And he also had to think about what getting involved with him meant for her. Whether either of them liked it or not, he was still a man with a prison record and more baggage than she'd probably expected or wanted. But he could give her little girl a happy memory.

After Adam was in position, Sage untied the bandana, and Jenna's eyes and mouth opened wide. The room was decorated with wildflowers, some lit candles, and pink and white streamers left over from the little girl's birthday party a few months ago.

"Hey, Little Bird, can you read the sign?"

She nodded and read it slowly, pointing at and sounding out each word. "It thays, 'W-W-Will . . . you . . . go . . . to . . . the . . . d-dan-danthe . . . w-with . . . me?'" Her eyes lit up as the meaning of the question sunk in. "You mean it?"

"Of course I do," Adam replied with a grin. "That's why I asked."

Spinning around to her mom with wide eyes, she clasped her hands together, bounced on the balls of her feet, and begged, "Can I, Mom? Can I go to the danth with Adam? *Pleathe, pleathe!*"

Sage laughed. "It's *may I*, and yes, you may go."

The little girl squealed in delight, turned back, and ran into his open arms. As he hugged her, he glanced up, saw Sage wiping away a runaway tear, and gave her a reassuring wink. The father/daughter dance crisis had been averted—now, he just had to have Sage teach him how to dance over the next three days.

———— ♥ ————

93

PUSHING A BUTTON ON THE SPEAKERS, SAGE ACTIVATED HER attached iPod, and the first of several easy-listening songs she'd put in a playlist came on. The soulful strains of "Strawberry Wine" by Deena Carter filled the barn. It was one of Sage's favorite songs and always reminded her of when she and Mark had first started dating back in college.

While Maddie was in the house getting the children ready for bed, Sage steeled herself to teach Adam how to dance. She was grateful to him for offering to take Jenna to the dance, but the last thing she wanted to do right now was step into his arms and let their bodies sway to the music. It would make her want things she couldn't have—namely, him—in her life . . . in her bed . . . in her heart.

Sage stood in the middle of the new floor, with the horses watching them curiously, and Adam followed her lead, stopping two feet away, facing her. Her stomach flip-flopped when he gave her a sweet grin. "Please forgive me in advance if I step on your toes. The last time I danced was at my senior prom, and even then, I wasn't good at it."

"Mark had two left feet when I first met him, so no worries. It's easier if we start at this distance . . ." She gestured between them. ". . . so you can look down and follow my feet at first." What she didn't add was that it would be less time in his arms too. While she was drawn to him in a way she'd only been with one other man in her life, she had her children to think about. Sage knew Adam would never hurt Jenna and Matthew intentionally—of that she was one hundred percent sure—but what would the other kids and people in town say about her being in a relationship with an ex-convict? Yes, he shouldn't have even gone to prison, but the facts always get lost when people start slinging mud—especially in their small town.

"Okay." Adam nodded and glanced down at her feet. "Let's do it."

She took his hands and placed one on her shoulder and the other on her waist. "We'll start with a simple box step. You step forward, and I'll step back, then one step to your right, then back and to the left."

He grinned at her. "I think your definition of simple is different than mine, but I'm willing to give it a shot."

Trying to ignore the heat from his palms permeating her clothing and skin, Sage led Adam in a basic dance. He was awkward and stiff at first and true to his prediction of stepping on her toes a few times, but as the sultry song wore on, he relaxed more and more. Unfortunately, that only made Sage's desire grow stronger. Their bodies swayed in time to the music, their steps growing shorter while the distance between them slowly dissipated. They'd started out a good eighteen inches away from each other, but by the time the first song ended and another began, their torsos and hips were almost touching. Sage kept her gaze pinned to Adam's chest, afraid of what would happen if she stared into his eyes. What little restraint she was holding onto was sure to vanish.

If Adam sensed her turmoil, he didn't show it. Instead, he brought her other hand up to rest on his shoulder, then wrapped his arms around her, closing the gap between them. Neither spoke—they just danced. The second song ended, and a third began. Sage no longer had the strength to hold him at bay. Lifting her chin, she found him gazing down at her. The sensual heat in his eyes matched that in her core. His full mouth almost begged to be kissed. Her hands slid up into his hair and tugged him toward her. Ever so slowly, Adam's face descended until their lips brushed against each other.

Sage groaned. Her hardened nipples were crushed against his chest, and she wanted to part her legs to let him grind his erection into her pelvis. Her need rose higher and higher as his tongue swept inside her mouth, tasting her cautiously. One would think an inexperienced, middle-aged man wouldn't be able to turn her on as much as this one did, but holy hell, the knowledge made her feel empowered.

The backs of her legs hit a stack of three hay bales, though she didn't remember being moved across the room. Still kissing her, Adam clutched her hips and lifted until she sat atop the hay. Parting her knees, she gave him room to settle between them. Whether the man knew it or not, he was seducing her. She wondered if she would have been so attracted and responsive had he come on like gangbusters instead of a shy, stray dog learning to trust and figuring out what was and wasn't allowed. She'd always had a soft spot for strays—damn it.

Grabbing his wrists, Sage dragged his hands up her torso and to her aching bosom. She moaned into his mouth and then sucked on his tongue as he tested the weight of her breasts, exploring and arousing her further. Leaving her mouth, he peppered kisses along her jawline to her ear. She pulled his navy-blue T-shirt from his jeans and tucked her hands underneath. His abdomen muscles quivered as she ran her fingertips upward. His skin was satin over hardened steel as she explored every dip and curve of his magnificent torso.

Adam's attention returned to her mouth, and he plunged his tongue inside. She couldn't get enough of him or remember why it was a bad idea to get involved with him. All that mattered was how he made her feel at this exact moment in time. She wrapped her legs around his hips and pulled him closer until his denim-covered cock rubbed against her core through her own jeans. They both moaned at the contact.

He took hold of her ponytail and tugged her head back, exposing her neck. His lips found her carotid pulse, and he licked and nibbled the skin covering it, sending her already thumping heart rate skyrocketing.

A faint rumbling filtered through Sage's brain, but it wasn't until a third round of thunder that the sound penetrated her sex-filled thoughts. This time, she groaned in dismay, and so did Adam. The pregnant mares and new foals needed to be brought back into the barn before the storm got any closer. Adam straightened and cupped her chin. His gaze pierced hers, and she could see how much he regretted having to stop. He placed a chaste peck on her nose. "Looks like playtime is over. Thanks for the dance lesson."

She couldn't help the coy smile that spread across her face. "It was my pleasure."

A deep chuckle came from his belly as he stepped back and helped her down. "Mine too."

Chapter Nine

Pushing her shopping cart, Sage strode up and down the aisles of the local Piggly Wiggly and checked things off her short list as she found them. She was only getting the necessities today as it would be another two weeks before the first two foals would be officially sold and the money deposited into her bank account. While she always felt sad saying goodbye to the horses, her family needed the money more than anything. Such was life on a farm.

As she made her way through the Health & Beauty aisle, she slowed as she came to the family planning section. Condoms weren't on her list and hadn't been since she'd first been married. But thoughts of Adam and how their private encounters had turned steamy lately—brief but steamy—she wondered when they would take things further and if Adam would think of needing protection. Sage was getting to the point where she was tempted to throw caution to the wind and tackle the man. Each brush of his lips against hers, each heated stare when no one was watching, and each touch that was far from innocent had her craving him.

Since his first dance lesson last week, she'd gone to bed alone and taken things into her own hands, so to speak, getting herself off to fantasies of him every night. She knew he was unaccustomed to romantic relationships, and they'd agreed to take things slow, but she was burning with need inside, and she desperately wanted him to put out the fire.

Out of the corner of her eye, she saw Mrs. Davidson, the church organist, coming her way, so Sage shifted her stance and gaze to the mini-pad and tampon section next to the condom display. There was no need to fuel the notorious gossip's fodder with a new rumor.

The two women exchanged pleasantries, but thankfully the old biddy moved along without her usual chitchat. As soon as Mrs. Davidson turned the corner at the end of the aisle, Sage snatched a box of condoms from the shelf and glanced around to confirm no one was nearby before hiding the prophylactics under a loaf of bread in her cart. Thank goodness, the store now had several self-checkout registers, so she wouldn't have to hand them to a clerk.

Quickly locating most of the items still on her list, Sage turned down the dairy aisle and stopped short. Standing a few feet away, Mrs. Davidson was conversing with Missy Brooks and Shelly Barrett, who were closer to Sage's age, and it was clear from their startled expressions she'd caught them off guard. Eyes widened and mouths dropped as they stared at her. Even if she hadn't heard the words "shacking up with an ex-con" fall from Missy's lips, it wasn't hard to figure out she'd interrupted their bull session concerning her and Adam.

Her eyes narrowed at the three gossip-mongers as she crossed her arms over her chest. "Please, don't stop talking on my account. I'm dying to hear all about the ex-con I'm shacking up with. I hate getting news third-hand, especially when it's about me and I should be the first to know. Tell me, how far has the rumor mill gotten? Have I given him a blowjob yet, or did we just fuck like rabbits?"

Mrs. Davidson gasped and brought her oh-so-holy-and-innocent hand to her chest as all three women blushed. The church organist was the first to recover. "W-Well, I never—"

"Maybe that's your problem then. Try getting laid, and maybe you'll find something juicier to do than talk about other people. Now, if you'll excuse me . . ." She pulled the condom box out from under the bread and waved it in their shocked faces. ". . . me and my *ex-con* have plans tonight."

Without giving them a chance to respond, Sage shoved her cart forward, forcing the women to jump out of her way. "Have a nice day, *ladies.*"

Her anger pulsated in her veins, and she fought hard to keep it under control. Pelting the women with containers of yogurt and sour cream like she wanted to would only be childish and give them more to talk about, no matter how satisfying it would be.

Damn it. She should have known that she and Adam would be the talk of the town after the barn raising when she'd kissed him in front of everyone, but it still bothered her—not that she'd let anyone know it. She'd gone from being Mark Hammond's poor widow to the town floozy in a scant few weeks, despite the fact her relationship with Adam hadn't been sealed in the biblical sense.

Grabbing two gallons of milk and the string cheese Jenna loved, Sage made sure that was all she needed from her list. She then headed toward the registers without a backward glance at the three bitches who probably already had their cell phones out and were texting or calling their rumor mill contacts. Well, it wasn't the first time she'd been in the line of fire of small-town gossip, and she doubted it would be her last.

Sage had always thought of herself as a strong and confident person, and when Mark had died, she had thankfully been able to draw on that strength. Before the children had come along, she'd worked side by side with her husband on the ranch and learned everything needed to run it efficiently, from the care of the animals to balancing the books. She'd met many contacts in the breeding world, so when it came to her making the calls to promote the new bloodlines, they'd already been familiar with her, and she'd earned their respect.

However, with Adam easing his way into her heart, she was getting used to having a man around again—a strong man she could lean on when times got tough. A lover who would hold her at night and keep her safe while reminding her she was a woman in her prime. A life partner she could love. But was Adam really that man? Or would she wake up one day and find him gone? Maybe if she gave him a reason to stay, he would.

She could no longer deny that she wanted Adam—in more ways than one. She would always love Mark, but he wouldn't have wanted her to spend the rest of her life alone and mourning him. If there really was an afterlife with conscious thought, maybe her husband had sent Adam to her because he couldn't be there himself. Well, whatever the reason Adam was there, it was time to let him know her feelings and see if he felt the same way in return.

Sage, darlin', it's time to up the ante and show the man what he'd be missing if he did walk away, and then maybe he wouldn't want to.

———— ❤ ————

Wiping his brow, Adam grabbed two bottles of water from the cooler in the bed of Evan's truck and poured one into an aluminum bowl for Benji, who'd been lying in the shade of the vehicle. It was ninety-six degrees outside a week before the July 4th holiday, and they expected another row of storms to be rolling through soon. The sky was getting dark, and Adam estimated he had about another fifteen minutes before he needed to pack up and head back to the barn. He and Evan had spent the morning repairing the fence line between Sage's property and Bart Sherman's, about sixty yards from where the land started to slope up into the tree-covered hills. This was the last section that needed replacement of the older wooden posts, which had recently begun to show signs of rot.

About an hour ago, after Sage had returned from the supermarket, Maddie had driven the boss's truck out to where the men were working and picked up Evan. He had a doctor's appointment for an annual checkup, and, according to his wife, he would have conveniently forgotten about it if she didn't drag him there herself. Apparently, the older man hated doctors.

Downing the whole bottle of water, Adam put the cap back on and tossed it into the bed next to the cooler as he eyed the approaching storm. The dark clouds reminded him of a conversation he'd had with Evan the other day.

"Do we get many tornadoes around here?" he'd asked. "I noticed the outdoor cellar behind my cottage and assume that's what it's for."

Evan had shaken his head. "We're lucky in this area. The last one that even came close to here was about twenty years ago, and it was still about fifteen miles away. Maddie and I were actually lucky that day. We were in Walmart when the sirens went off. Everyone was huddled in the back of the store when we heard that monster come roaring in. The building shook but stayed standing. And just like that, it was over. When we got outside, all the stores on the opposite side of the highway were destroyed—on our side, there was a ton of debris in the parking lots but no damage to the buildings. I always said it was like God flipped a coin, and the other side of the highway lost. How two people were the only ones killed was beyond me."

Adam had heard similar analogies in the past. It was hard for people to understand how a person, standing in the wrong place at the wrong time, died while someone two feet away was spared.

This would be the third string of storms within a week. Thankfully, it had been clear skies for Jenna's dance the other night. The elementary school cafeteria had been transformed into a pink, white, and purple fantasy ballroom for the young girls and their fathers or father figures. It had given Adam an opportunity to socialize with other men from the small town. He'd met quite a few during the two-day barn raising and had been introduced to others at the dance.

While most of the new acquaintances had been friendly enough toward him, there had been a few who'd eyed him with distrust for most of the evening. Chris Miller, Ashley's husband, who'd hung out with him for most of the dance while his daughter, Lucy, played with Jenna, had told him just to give those people the middle finger, but Adam had passed on the suggestion. Their negative attitudes toward him hadn't been anything unexpected, and as long as Jenna had a good time, nothing else mattered to him. He was learning to live with the proverbial scarlet letter on his chest.

After the quick water break, Adam finished repairing the last of the fence line, and just in time. The rain was about a mile out, and he could see it crossing Bart Sherman's expansive property. Lightning flashed in the distance. He had to hurry if he was going to beat the storm back to the house.

Adam gathered up his tools and placed them with the old, rotted posts in the truck bed. He bent down to pick up the remaining roll of fence wire when something struck the dirt next to it, sending a puff of dust into the air. A split second later, he heard the rifle shot.

Someone's shooting at me!

Leaving the large spool where it sat, Adam dove toward the pickup truck just as another bullet struck where he'd been a split second earlier. Ducking behind the engine block, he tried to assess what was happening. There shouldn't be any hunters up in the woods, which meant it was no accident. If he were a gambling man, he'd bet everything he had that a sniper was aiming at him.

"Benji! Come here, boy!" The dog obeyed immediately and ran to Adam's side. "Good boy. Stay."

A close crack of thunder nearly had Adam jumping out of his skin, thinking there was another shooter to the west of him. Even Benji startled and whined but stayed next to Adam. If they didn't get out of there soon, he and the dog would be sitting ducks for not only the maniac up in the woods but for the bolts of lightning looking for something to strike.

Taking a chance at getting shot in the foot under the

truck, Adam crab-crawled forward so he could open the door, then retrieve Evan's phone from the middle console and a loaded rifle from the rack behind the seats. Grabbing the cell, he almost dropped it when the driver's window exploded, peppering him with shattered glass.

"Shit!" Snatching the rifle from its perch, he slammed the door shut and huddled behind the engine block. Benji practically glued his furry self against Adam's thigh. "Damn, fucking bastard!"

And wasn't that a freaking hoot? All that time in prison, and it took getting shot at to have him cursing like a figurative sailor. If he survived the next few minutes, he'd make sure he got to confession this week with the good reverend.

Dialing 9-1-1, he prayed Sage or the kids were safe back at the main house.

"9-1-1, what is your emergency?" a bored female voice asked.

"This is Adam Westfield out at Heaven's Pastures. There's a sniper in the north woods shooting at me."

"A sniper? You mean a hunter?"

He almost rolled his eyes. "No, I mean a sniper has shot at me three times. Send patrol out here and tell them to be careful."

"Hold, please."

Pulling the phone from his ear, he stared at it incredulously.

She put me on hold? Seriously?

Adam dropped to his knees, leaned down, and peeked under the truck to see if anyone had emerged from the tree line.

So far, so good.

Fat raindrops inched closer until he felt them on his back, but his attention was split between watching for the sniper and waiting for the damn operator to get back on the line. No more gunfire sounded, but the thunder and lightning were getting closer.

When the phone line clicked, it wasn't the female dispatcher again. "This is Sheriff Cosgrove. Who's this?"

He was pretty sure the man knew exactly who was on the line before getting on the phone because his animosity toward Adam was glaringly clear. "Adam Westfield. I'm at Sage's ranch, and there's a sniper up in the north woods shooting at me."

"Probably a hunter. I doubt it's anything to worry about unless it's one of your old prison buddies paying you a visit."

Anger coursed through him as his tone of voice grew louder and harsher. "Are you freaking kidding me? Listen, Cosgrove . . ." He intentionally left off the man's title. ". . . it's not a damn hunter. Get your men out here and now! Sage and her kids are on the property, and if something happens to one of them, there'll be hell to pay. Understood?"

A harrumph came over the line, but thankfully, the man no longer argued with him. "I'll send someone over."

The call disconnected, and he fought the urge to throw the phone. By the time the sheriff got off his lazy ass and sent someone to investigate, Adam could be dead. Leaning down in the mud that had quickly developed, he scanned the expanse between the truck and the bottom of the hill leading up into the woods again. Another bolt of lightning streaked across the sky with the crack of thunder a split second behind it. Adam couldn't wait anymore. He had to risk a run for it.

Opening the passenger door again, he kept as low as possible and crawled into the truck. He held onto the rifle and slid across the bench seat, ignoring the thousands of tiny glass pieces. Calling for Benji to jump in after him, he turned the key while trying to make himself as small a target as possible by ducking away from the open space where the driver's window used to be. The engine roared to life as the now soaking-wet dog hid in the passenger foot area. Without closing the passenger door—the truck's momentum would do that for him—Adam threw the vehicle in gear and gunned the accelerator. The tires spun momentarily before finding traction and hurtling across the pasture. The tailgate was still down, and some of the posts and tools flew off the back of the bed, but that was the least of his worries.

Between the deluge of rain pounding on the truck roof and coming in the broken window, and the thunder roaring overhead, he couldn't be certain, but it appeared the sniper had ceased his ambush. However, Adam wasn't taking any chances. The speeding vehicle bounced hard as it ate up the land between the northwest pasture and Sage's house, and Adam prayed he didn't bust an axle or anything else underneath. Moments later, he skidded to a stop next to the main barn under the metal roof of an outdoor horse stall, so the truck's interior wouldn't get flooded. Grabbing the rifle off the seat, he threw the door open. "C'mon, boy!"

The two made a mad dash to the back porch of the house, which didn't stop them from getting soaked. Adam yanked open the screen door as Sage did the same to the interior one. Staring at him, her eyes widened as he bolted into the kitchen, gun in hand and Benji on his heels. Man and dog ignored the fact they were leaving puddles in their wake.

Sage closed the storm door. "Wh-what's wrong? Are you okay? I saw you racing in."

"Where are the kids?" he barked, more concerned for their safety than he was about his tone of voice at the moment.

"In their rooms. Adam, what's wrong?"

Reaching around her, he locked the backdoor before striding through the house and setting the deadbolt on the front door. Lowering his voice, so the children wouldn't hear him, he said, "Someone was shooting at me from the trees above the northwest pasture."

"What? Oh, my God! Are you sure? Were you hit?" Her gaze and hands frantically inspected him for signs of blood.

Adam placed a reassuring yet shaking hand on her shoulder. Trying to slow his adrenaline-fueled pulse, he hoped she'd be convinced when he said, "*Shh*, Sage. I'm fine, and so is Benji. Just soaking wet, that's all. And yes, I'm positive I was the target." The dog decided at that moment to shake the rain from his body, sending water flying in every direction, and Adam wished he could do the same. He was soaked to the skin. "I called 9-1-1, and the sheriff is sending some deputies over, although I'm sure the guy is long gone. The driver's window of Evan's truck is long gone too."

"You could've been killed." She was still in shock and making sure he wasn't bleeding, but at least she was now talking in a hushed tone. "Oh, my God! Why was someone shooting at you?"

"I have no idea, but you better believe I'm going to find out. Go check on the kids and get your pistol until the cavalry shows up." He nudged her toward the hallway before returning to the kitchen. From the window over the sink, he could observe a good portion of the property to monitor anyone approaching. Benji would bark as usual if a vehicle came up the long driveway in front of the house.

Adam glanced at the kitchen clock. Maddie and Evan would return soon, and he had to warn them. Finding Maddie's number in the phone he still had on him, he pressed send and waited for the call to be picked up.

"Hello?" Maddie never picked up the phone while she was driving, so she was either in the passenger seat or they were still at Evan's appointment.

"Maddie, it's Adam. Are you still at the doctor's?"

"We're on our way home. Do you need something from town?"

"No," he answered as Sage rushed back into the kitchen with her loaded pistol in her hand, aiming it at the floor. She must have told the children to stay in their rooms for now. "I need to talk to Evan. Tell him to pull over and give him the phone."

"All—all right." The woman clearly figured out something was wrong.

Adam heard Maddie tell her husband what he'd said. Seconds passed, and then the older man came on the line. "What's wrong, son?"

Sometime during the last few weeks of working together and having long talks about a multitude of subjects, Evan had taken to calling him "son" occasionally, and it reminded Adam of his foster father. The two men would probably have become good friends if Harry was still alive.

"Don't come home yet. Someone was shooting at me up in the northwest from the woods."

"What! Are you—"

"I'm fine," Adam assured him. "I'm back at the house with Sage and the kids waiting for the damn sheriff to send his men over here. I just don't want you pulling in until the deputies arrive."

"Son of a—" This time, Evan cut himself off in mid-sentence. "Well, those idiots are on their way now. They just passed us by Davidson's farm stand." That was about three miles away from the turnoff for Heaven's Pasture. "No damn lights or sirens, though. They look like they're out for a goddamn Sunday drive. You got my rifle?"

"Yes, sir. And our pistol packin' mama is locked and loaded too." Despite the severity of the situation, he gave Sage a smile and a wink.

"Good. We'll be home in a few minutes, son. Hang tight."

Hanging up, Adam checked the window again as Sage went to the front of the house to wait for the sheriff's deputies to pull in. Thankfully, it wasn't long before two patrol cars came up the drive. Adam joined Sage in the foyer and opened the door. Cosgrove climbed out of one and a deputy from the other, then dashed to the front porch through the pouring rain. From the scowl on the sheriff's face, it was evident he was pissed and thought this was a complete waste of time. Removing their wide-brimmed hats, the two men stepped inside.

"Now, what's this all about, Westfield?" the sheriff growled with annoyance while eying the rifle Adam still had cradled in his arms.

He bit the inside of his cheek to keep from decking the arrogant man and handed the weapon to Sage, who still had her pistol in her other hand. The last thing he wanted was for either of the lawmen to be nervous that an ex-con was holding a loaded weapon, no matter what the situation. Crossing his arms, he glared at Cosgrove. "Whether you believe me or not, Sherriff, someone was shooting at me in the northwest pasture. Just before the rain started. I was packing up the truck, and two shots missed my boots by inches. A third shot took out the driver's window of Evan's truck. There's a possibility the slug is still in the cab —I was too busy getting the hell out of there to check."

"Harrumph. Did you see anyone? If the slug isn't in the vehicle, I doubt there'll be any other evidence to be found. Kind of convenient that it happened right before the downpour, which would probably wash away any evidence."

Adam clenched his fist. Now he desperately wanted to punch the man's smirk off his face. But that would land him in jail.

Boots on the porch caught all their attention, and the door swung open. Maddie's face was filled with worry as she visually inspected Adam and then Sage. Evan was right behind her with a similar expression. "You all right, son?"

Nodding, Adam stepped further into the living room since there wasn't enough space for all of them in the foyer. "Yeah, but your truck needs a new driver's window."

"That's what insurance is for." Evan glared at the two uniformed men. "Sheriff, what are you going to do about this?"

"About what? It was probably some hunter, and Westfield is blowing it out of proportion."

Standing beside Adam, Sage sputtered as her face turned red. "W-what? You can't be serious, Sheriff! First, someone torches my barn, and now someone is shooting at my ranch hand, and you think he's blowing it out of proportion? You're fucking crazy!"

"Sage, *shhh*, the kids." Adam placed a hand on her back and rubbed it from side to side. He felt her stiffen for a split second, then some of the tension eased from her body, and she leaned into his touch. His heart rate increased, and he suddenly wished they were alone.

After hanging up her raincoat, Maddie bustled past the

others toward the hallway. "I'll take care of the children while the sheriff and the deputy do their jobs and take a detailed report, followed by a full investigation. Being this is an election year and all."

Subtle the woman was not, and Adam fought the urge to laugh. But her veiled threat had the desired effect on the others as everyone relaxed a little more, even if the sheriff still appeared annoyed. The man wrapped his big hand around the doorknob. "Prescott, take the report, then when the rain stops, have Westfield show you the truck and where it all went down. Log in any evidence if you find it. I'll send Miller out to help."

Cosgrove either didn't give a shit or thought it was a hoax, but at least something was being done. After the man hurried back out to his vehicle and drove away, Sage let out a heavy sigh, then smiled warmly at the young deputy. "Come into the kitchen, Brian. You can take Adam's report there, and I'll put some coffee on for everyone."

An hour later, with the sun now shining again, Miller and Prescott left with the one slug which had been found lodged into the passenger door of Evan's truck. Unfortunately, the rain had washed away any other sign of the sniper or the first two shots.

As Maddie and Sage prepared dinner and Evan fed the animals, Adam strode back to his cottage. He needed a shower and some dry clothes.

Closing the door behind him, he leaned against it and shut his eyes. His body began to tremble as he finally let it react to the terror he'd felt earlier, which he'd kept hidden from the others. It wasn't what could've happened to him that had him so worried but to Sage, the children, and the Tanners. It hadn't escaped his notice that it wouldn't have been difficult for someone on Bart Sherman's land to ride up on horseback into the woods and then cross over until they were above Sage's property to shoot at him. Maybe it was time to find out all he could about Sherman and why the man had been doggedly trying to get the property that had been in Mark Hammond's family for generations.

Chapter Ten

S miling softly, Sage put the items back into Mark's memory box one by one. It had been a bittersweet trip into the past. There were pictures, ticket stubs, a four-leaf clover they'd found on a picnic one day, the pen they'd used to sign their marriage license, little love notes they'd given each other, and a whole bunch of other things which only had sentimental value for the two of them. Anyone else looking through the contents would see most of it as useless junk.

Once everything was neatly packed away again, she stared at the contents for a moment before her gaze fell on the simple, gold wedding band on her left ring finger. Since Mark's death, she hadn't imagined ever wanting to take it off—never thought she'd meet someone who made her want to take it off. But that had changed. Whether she and Adam had something special growing between them or not, whether he was here to stay or if he'd be moving on someday, it was time for Sage to admit she had a full life still yet to lead.

Sliding the ring from her finger, she brought it to her

lips and kissed it before placing it in the box with all the other items. When they were old enough, maybe Jenna would like to wear it when she got married, or Matthew would like to give it to his bride. The fact that she wasn't crying as she shut the box lid told Sage she'd made the right decision. It was time to move on.

Sage stood and placed the box in the top drawer of her dresser, then pulled on her knee-length silk robe over its matching nightgown as her insecurity battled with her body's wants and needs. When she'd heard how close Adam had come to being killed today, she realized she'd fallen in love with him—not still *falling*, but *fallen*, as in a done deal, and her mind, body, and heart were all in agreement. He really was a good man . . . a man she could give herself to. And, hopefully, he would give himself to her in return.

Pushing her feet into her slippers, she stepped out into the hallway and listened outside the doors to the children's bedrooms. Jenna was snoring softly, and when Sage peeked into Matthew's room, she saw he was passed out too. Following dinner, Evan and Maddie had stayed for a while, and they'd all played some board games, trying to erase the nervous energy in the house the kids had obviously been picking up on. Afterward, Jenna and Matthew had fallen asleep during the first ten minutes of a movie they'd begged to watch. Adam had carried the two and put them into their beds for Sage before softly kissing her goodnight and leaving for his cottage with the rifle Evan had insisted he keep. The older man had several other weapons at home for him and Maddie to stay safe.

What would he say if she knocked on his door and, when he opened it, slid the robe from her body? Would he turn her down—premarital sex and all that—or would he pull her into his arms and give her everything she begged for? Only one way to find out. She couldn't deny what she craved anymore and just hoped he felt the same way.

Opening the backdoor, Sage bravely put one foot in front of the other and soon found herself on Adam's doorstep. Taking a deep breath, she let it out, then lifted her hand and knocked. Seconds ticked by before the door swung open, and there he stood in all his handsome glory. A five o'clock shadow covered his jawline and upper lip. Unlike the first time she'd observed him in the cottage through the window, he was wearing gray cotton shorts that hung low on his hips instead of lounge pants, probably in deference to the warmer weather. But like that first night, it was all he was wearing—no shirt, no shoes, no problem. If he turned her down, maybe he wouldn't mind if she just stood there all night, drooling over his muscular body.

"Sage? Something wrong?"

"Hmm?" Apparently, drooling over him was exactly what she was doing. Her gaze left his well-defined six-pack and chest to look him in the eye. He raised an eyebrow at her, and she shook the lack-of-sex-induced cobwebs from her mind. "No. Nothing's wrong. Um . . . may I come in?"

The confusion in his eyes morphed into heat as he moved to the side, opening the door wider for her to enter. Swallowing her nervousness, Sage stepped forward, and the door closed behind her. A sensual shiver snaked up her spine as she spun around slowly to find him leaning against the jamb, watching her every move.

Electricity seemed to crackle about the room as they studied each other in silence. Sage realized that she needed to make the first move here. She took a step toward him, her voice a husky whisper. "Please don't send me away."

Placing her hand on his bare chest, she stared at their physical connection, and he inhaled sharply. She let his warmth seep into her palm. His pectoral muscles twitched, and his heart rate increased under her touch. "I need you."

Adam's hand came up and covered hers. Sage lifted her chin until their gazes met—the desire in his eyes set her hormones in overdrive. Reaching up with his other hand, he cupped her jaw, his fingers curving around to the back of her neck. He pulled her near. "I need you too, Sage. I couldn't send you away, even if it cost me my next breath."

His head descended, and he kissed her gently . . . tentatively. Sage placed her other hand next to the first, then slid both up to his shoulders, reveling in how soft his skin was over the strength in the muscles just beneath it. Drawing her closer, he deepened the kiss. His tongue darted out and licked the seam of her mouth. Unable to resist, she parted her lips, inviting him in. Adam groaned as he tasted and drank her in. Her body was flush against his, and she could feel his cock lengthen in his shorts. She ran a hand through his hair, which was damp as if he'd been in the shower moments earlier, and the thought of him all naked, wet, and soapy made her clit throb.

Without breaking the kiss, he bent his knees and swept her up into his arms. His bare feet slapped against the wooden floor until they hit the carpet in his bedroom. He lowered her legs until she stood again, then slowly withdrew his mouth from hers. There was no mistaking the desire on his face, but it was mixed with uncertainty. A soft, warm glow from the small lamp on the nightstand illuminated the room, and fresh yet humid air, leftover from his shower, filtered out from the open bathroom door.

This time when his hands cupped her jaw, she felt them

quiver. "Sage. I want to make this good for you. Show me how. Tell me how to touch you—how to please you."

Biting her bottom lip, she wrapped her hands around his wrists and pushed downward, stopping when his fingers found the tie to her floral, pink robe. His gaze never left hers as he tugged on one end, releasing the knot. The two sides fell away, revealing the matching nightgown underneath. Sage shrugged off the robe and let it pool at her feet.

A glance down at Adam's prominent erection, tenting his shorts, had her feeling emboldened. A seductive kitten —one she'd thought had long since disappeared from within her—emerged. Lifting one hand, she brought it to her opposite shoulder and pushed the thin strap of the nightgown down onto her upper arm. She then repeated the same action on the other side. A firestorm flared in Adam's eyes as she dropped her arms, allowing the silken material to slide down her body to the floor. His breath caught, stoking the inferno blazing in her core. He pushed his shorts down from his hips to join her discarded clothing. His cock was a thing of beauty—satin over steel, thick veins running the length of it, a dark purple flush at the tip.

Taking his hands, she lifted them to her breasts and covered them with her own hands. Squeezing his palms and fingers around the lush orbs, she showed him how she liked to be touched. How she *needed* to be touched.

Letting one of his hands go, she held the other in place and stepped back until her legs hit the bed. Adam followed as she climbed onto the mattress and lay beside her. His lips descended on hers again as his fingers plucked and rolled her nipple. Sage ran her hands over every inch of him she could reach.

When she brushed against his erection, he hissed, and

his hips bucked as he tore his mouth from hers. "Woman, as much as I want you to wrap your hand around me, I think if you did, this would be over in seconds, and neither of us wants that to happen." He shifted further down on the bed. "Let me explore you."

Before she could answer, he kissed, licked, and nibbled on her neck, collarbones, and the top swell of her breasts. Whenever she moaned, gasped, or squirmed, he repeated whatever he'd done to elicit the involuntary response from her body. Sucking a nipple into his mouth, he laved it with his tongue. Sage's hand went to the back of his head and clutched his hair, keeping him on task. Grasping his other hand, she dragged it down her torso and lower still to the part of her that was pleading to be stroked. With her fingers on top of his, she showed him how to please her . . . how to take her higher.

Sage had begun masturbating again these past few weeks as her body had finally joined her mind in the land of the living. But this was better than she could ever do on her own. The callouses on Adam's fingertips felt like heaven over her clitoris and labia. Her index finger pressed his into her wet core, and her hips rose off the bed as need coursed through her.

As Adam began to plunge in and out of her wet channel without encouragement, Sage ran her fingers over the tip of his shaft, finding a pearl of cream. Remembering what he'd said about things being over far too soon, if she wrapped her hand around him, she decided to explore the rest of his body. Her palms caressed every inch of him she could reach. As much as she wanted him inside her, she also didn't want to rush this. It'd been two and a half years since she'd been intimate with a man, and she wanted to savor every moment of it.

Adam left her breast and shifted to give its twin the same attention. Reaching down, Sage fingered her clit as he teased her swollen labia and learned what made her gasp, moan his name, and beg for more. "Oh, Adam! Yessss! More! Don't stop!"

Her hips undulated when his fingers thrust back inside her. "Oh! Right there! Again!" He'd brushed over that spot that sent her barreling toward the edge of a cliff. When he rubbed it repeatedly at her command, she knew there was no stopping the orgasm that began in her core and rippled outward. Black spots swam before her closed eyelids, and her mouth gaped as she keened with her release. Clutching his shoulders, her nails dug into his skin, and her body shook while she clenched around his fingers.

As she floated back down, Sage gulped lungfuls of air and slowly opened her eyes to find Adam hovering over her, staring down at her face. Her mouth turned up in a sated smile. "Like riding a bike."

A deep, throaty chuckle came from him. "I guess so."

His erection bobbed against her stomach, and she glanced down. A blush stole across her cheeks. "There's . . . um . . . I picked up some . . . um . . . condoms the other day . . . just—just in case . . . I mean . . . I wasn't sure—"

"Where are they?" His words sounded as if someone was strangling his throat, and she knew he was barely hanging on by a thread.

"The—the pocket of my robe."

Pushing off from the mattress, Adam retrieved the garment from the floor and found the small foil squares she'd placed in the right pocket. Holding them up, he raised his eyebrows at her. "Three? Your confidence in me might be a little overindulgent."

Sage giggled. "We won't know until we try."

Dropping the robe and tossing two of the condoms onto the nightstand, Adam ripped the third one open and removed the latex disk. As Sage watched through heavy-lidded eyes, he fumbled briefly before rolling it over his prominent shaft. Once he was prepared, he crawled back onto the bed, but this time between her legs. Sage spread them wider for him.

"You're beautiful . . . simply beautiful," he said while his tender gaze roamed her face. "I think I should have told you that earlier."

Her blush deepened. "Well, your mouth was pretty busy earlier."

"That it was." His expression turned serious and apologetic. "I'm not going to last long, Sage. I'll be shocked if I don't explode the moment I'm inside you."

Reaching up, she ran her hand over his whiskered jaw. "It's okay. We have all night and two more condoms if that happens. Come here."

Taking hold of his hips, she urged him to lower himself down on top of her. His pelvis settled between her upper thighs as he brushed his lips against hers. "I just want it to be good for you."

"It already has been, Adam. From the moment you kissed me. Make love to me so that it can be good for both of us."

Snaking her hand between them, she used her fingers to guide him. As the tip of his cock penetrated her, she felt him stiffen. His eyes were closed tightly, and he was biting his bottom lip so hard she was afraid he'd draw blood. Her body yielded to him as he eased his way in with short, purposeful strokes. He gasped, then tensed again. "Feels . . . damn! It feels incredible. You feel incredible."

"So do you," Sage whispered. "Don't hold back, Adam."

His response to her words was as if someone had fired a starter pistol. He rocked his hips forward, then drew out of her core just to thrust back in. He filled her again and again, and the drag of him against her tight walls was intoxicating. Supporting most of his weight on his forearms on either side of her head, he tried to establish a rhythm but faltered several times. It took her a moment to realize he wanted to bring her to another orgasm, this time with him. But as good as he felt, she doubted that was going to happen this go-around. However, it was something to strive for next time.

Sage wrapped her legs around his hips, and the new angle sent him even further within her. "Don't wait for me, Adam. Come for me. Just let go."

"I—I . . . damn . . . I—*aarrrgghh*!" His muscles seized as he plunged deep a final time. His jaw clenched, and his eyelids slammed shut. His hips twitched a few times as he emptied himself inside the latex barrier.

She felt the tension begin to leave him as his lungs heaved for oxygen. Sweat coated his skin. When he finally opened his eyes and met hers, she thought she saw something she never expected to see in another man's gaze that was directed at her. She saw love. But when he spoke, there was no declaration that would have made her heart soar. Instead, he said, "I'm sorry, but going twenty years without, there was no way I could control myself. I wanted you to come with me. I'm sorry."

Pushing aside the thoughts of love, Sage brushed his damp temple with her fingertips. "Well, like they say . . . practice makes perfect."

His chuckle caused him to slide from her body, and he rolled off her onto his side. "Give this old man a break. It's going to be hours before I can do that again."

She gave him a saucy grin. "As long as you want to do it again, I can wait."

Putting his arms around her, he tucked her against his body. "Bless you, woman. Bless you."

———— ♥ ————

PUSHING THE EGGS AROUND ON HIS PLATE, ADAM TRIED TO conjure up an appetite, but there were way too many things on his mind—the main one being Sage and what they'd done last night. She'd left his bed around 4:00 a.m. to return to her own. He hadn't wanted her to leave, yet he'd been relieved when she had.

"You going to eat those eggs or puree them?" Reverend Stevens asked as he dipped a piece of toast in the gooey yolk of his poached eggs. "Or you could just spit out whatever's on your mind."

Adam glanced up at the salt-and-pepper-haired clergyman, then around the little diner where they were having breakfast together. After feeding the animals this morning, he'd borrowed Sage's truck to run into town and pick up a few things. Somehow, it'd steered itself to the church he'd been attending each Sunday. Reverend Stevens had just finished preparing his sermon for the following day, and Adam had invited him to grab something to eat. But now that they were sitting there, Adam had no clue what he wanted to say to the man.

He sighed and left his fork on the plate, then picked up his coffee before putting it right back down again. Crossing his arms on the table, he leaned forward. The good reverend was the only person other than Sage in the town who knew most of the details of his past. "I'm in a bit of a conundrum, and I don't know what to do about it. I'm fighting feelings I never expected to have."

"You're falling for Sage." Adam's eyes shot up at the statement, and the man chuckled. "I may be a man of the cloth, Adam, but I'm not blind. That's one of the good things about being a Protestant minister—you're allowed to fall in love and marry your soul mate. After twenty-two years of marriage, Mrs. Stevens still makes my heart beat faster just by walking into the room. And I'm grateful for every day the Lord has given me with her."

Greta Stevens was a petite, round woman with a heart of gold. Adam had liked her immediately when he'd met her. He'd also seen the love in the couple's eyes whenever they looked at each other. Adam pursed his lips. "I'm afraid I'm not worthy of her. She's been through so much, and I'm worried I'll never measure up to her husband."

Taking a sip of his coffee, the reverend sat back in the booth with a look of contemplation on his face. "Mark was a good man . . . but so are you, Adam. I would never have recommended you go to Sage for a job if I didn't believe that in my heart. It's time to forgive yourself for what happened. Come your Judgment Day, I'm sure you'll find God has already forgiven you. Everyone has a past—good and bad—it's what makes us human. I don't think for a minute you don't regret what happened. Most men would have fought going to prison, but you accepted the sentence as your penance. I'm not sure I would have had the courage to do the same. Everyone has a choice on how to live their future, and their choices influence not only themselves but everyone around them."

Adam knew that. It was similar to something he'd told the other inmates in prison during the weekly prayer services. Adam checked their surroundings again to make sure no one was in earshot. They were sitting in a back booth, and most of the morning diners had finished their meals and left. "Can you hear my confession, Reverend?"

"Here?" Stevens glanced around. Adam had been to him several times to confess his sins since arriving in Rosewood, even though there were differences between the Catholic and Protestant teachings concerning confessionals. The reverend had no problem with a person of any religion coming to him for help in receiving God's forgiveness. "Certainly. I've had people come clean to me in stranger places."

A brief smile appeared on Adam's face before it quickly faded again. Making the sign of the cross on his face and his chest, he bowed his head. "Bless me, Reverend, for I have sinned. It's been one week since my last confession." He admitted his sins before ending with the one that had been troubling him the most. "Lastly, I've had sexual relations with a woman."

When the reverend didn't answer him, Adam glanced up to see the man had raised an eyebrow at him, but not in disappointment as expected. It wasn't hard for him to guess Adam had been talking about Sage—at least Stevens could be trusted to keep that information to himself. "And this is something you regret, son?"

"No. Yes. I mean . . ." He ran a hand through his hair in frustration. "I don't know what I mean."

Stevens leaned forward again, his voice full of under-standing. "Let me tell you something, Adam. I wasn't always a minister—in fact, there were times I wasn't even a church-goer. It wasn't until I was in my late twenties that I'd heard the calling while I was dating Greta, and she and I hadn't exactly been saints with our relationship up to that point if you get my drift. Again, we're human. And we'd already committed ourselves to each other even though we hadn't stood at the front of the church yet and professed it for everyone else to hear. If God hadn't intended for us to falter, how would we ever learn how much we need Him? You resigned from the Brotherhood. Therefore, you're not still bound by the rules of celibacy, so there's nothing to worry about with that. There are things in every religion that can be interpreted in different ways depending on any given person. If love and compassion are involved, I believe what happens between a couple behind closed doors is between them—if I didn't, I'd be a bit of a hypocrite. I assume this wasn't just a fling for you or a way to blow off steam."

Adam shook his head. "Not at all. I care about her . . . a lot. Heck, I think I'm in love with her, but again, how do I know if I'm worthy of her and her children?"

"Ask her," Stevens stated without hesitation.

"Huh?"

"Ask her. Who better to tell you if you're worthy or not than the woman herself?"

His smile returned. Sometimes it took someone stating the obvious for it to make sense in your head. Now Adam had to work up the courage to ask Sage how she felt and just hope her answer was one he could live with.

Chapter Eleven

"Hurry, Mommy! Hurry, Adam! I need to get my balloons!"

Jenna pulled on both their hands as she walked between them down Main Street. An eight-block strip of the primary thoroughfare had been shut down to traffic for the Fourth of July parade and carnival. Each year, a different town in the county hosted the summer celebration, and this year it was in Rosewood. The fire department had hung red, white, and blue banners across the street along the entire route, and several vendors were selling balloons, flags, and other patriotic items, which added to the festive atmosphere. The carnival was set up on the grounds of the elementary school's baseball and soccer fields at the opposite end of the strip from where Adam had parked Sage's truck. Despite the distance, he could see the Ferris wheel that Jenna had been begging him to take her on all morning.

Matthew was with Toby and the rest of their baseball teammates, who would be marching with all the other Little League teams, and Sage wanted to wait for them near the firehouse where the parade would end. While many greeted them warmly during their walk from the church parking lot a few blocks away, several people eyed Adam warily, and it was starting to piss Sage off. There was also a lot of whispering going on behind hands brought to the face. It was obvious word had spread about his being in prison. She still didn't know how it got out, but she wondered if Ashley had gone against her wishes and blurted out the secret. She mentally shook the thought from her head—if anyone had blabbed, it was probably Sheriff Cosgrove.

As Jenna tugged on their arms again, Sage tried to calm down the excited child. "Easy, sweetheart. There are plenty of balloons. I promise they won't run out."

"But I have to be thure they have red, white, and blue oneth. Adam thaid I could get all three."

Smiling, Adam squeezed the girl's hand. "That's right, Little Bird. But your mom is also right. There are plenty of them."

Jenna sighed like she had the weight of the world on her shoulders and the adults just didn't understand how important the red, white, and blue balloons were to the July 4th celebration. "Okay, but I'll be mad if they're all gone."

Sage grinned and shook her head in amusement as Adam chuckled. It was nice to see him relaxed—in fact, she was too. There hadn't been any more incidents at the ranch. Everything had been quiet since the day Adam had been shot at. The sheriff's deputies hadn't been able to find a lead on who the sniper had been, and the county forensic office had reported the slug that had been pulled from Evan's truck had been too damaged to be useful.

Every night since then, Sage had gone to Adam's cabin after Jenna and Matthew were asleep, and they'd spent several hours in his bed, exploring each other. However, she never stayed the whole night. She had no idea where this thing between them was going and was still afraid Adam would wake up one day and tell her it was time for him to move on. That was the main reason she'd insisted they keep their blossoming relationship to themselves, although it wasn't the reason she'd given him. For that, she'd told him it was for the children's sake. While it was true she was protecting them from getting their hopes up about anything, she was also trying to protect her own heart.

Yes, she'd fallen in love with him, but despite the sex, he still hadn't come anywhere near professing his love for her. She had no idea if she was just a stepping stone for him. Could he have ended up in any woman's bed sooner or later, and hers just happened to be available?

For now, she'd enjoy what Adam would give her, but she had to maintain a certain distance. Having him break her heart if he left was one thing, but letting him know he'd broken her heart was something completely different. He had to *want* to stay with her, and not because he felt guilty about anything.

Pushing all worries and doubts from her mind, she was determined to have a fun day. When they reached the first souvenir vendor, Adam let Jenna pick out her balloons, then bought different versions of patriotic hats for all three of them. Donning their hats, they quickly found a spot along the parade route where they could all see the marchers go by. The opening band could be heard as the mayor, riding in a beautifully restored, black 1955 Ford Thunderbird convertible, waved to the crowd as he led the parade. Forty-five minutes of marching bands, firemen, sheriff's deputies, mounted police, cheerleaders, Little Leaguers, veterans, flag bearers, and more followed.

After collecting Matthew and Toby, Sage and Adam followed the children through the crowd heading to the carnival. There, they found Maddie and Evan in the blue-ribbon tent, waiting for the judging to begin for several events. Evan was at one table, monitoring a large vat of Maddie's chili, while his wife was standing behind the table where her blueberry, blackberry, and peach cobbler pies were on display. Sage waved across the tent to where Ashley, Hilde, and two other women were currently having their lasagnas critiqued by the three judges. The winners would be announced after all the food tastings had finished.

"Mom! Can Toby and I go with Josh and his dad on some rides?"

"*May* Toby and I . . ." Sage admonished her son.

Matthew rolled his eyes and then bounced on the balls of his feet. "*May* Toby and I go with Josh and his dad?"

"Yes, as long as you pay attention to Mr. Garner and don't go running off on your own."

Sage had barely gotten the words out before the boys ran out of the tent. "We will!"

A bark of laughter escaped Adam. "Was that 'we will' for paying attention or running off on their own?"

"I hope it was for paying attention, but with those two, you never know."

Sage introduced Adam to several people as they walked around the tent with Jenna. When they reached Ashley's table, the little girl started squirming. "Mommy, I have to go to the baffroom."

"Okay, sweetheart." Sage took her daughter's hand. "Adam, we'll be right back."

———— ❤ ————

As they hurried away, Adam turned back to Ashley, took a deep breath, and let it out slowly. "Okay. Say what's on your mind before you blow a gasket. You don't like me."

She raised an eyebrow at him, clearly thrown by his straightforwardness. "Okay, I'll play. You're partially right. I think you're a nice enough guy—"

"But not nice enough for Sage," he finished for her.

"She's my best friend, Adam—I don't want her to get hurt. She suffered enough after she lost Mark."

He crossed his arms over his chest and leaned his hip against the table. "That's understandable. But the last thing I would do is hurt Sage or her children, Ashley. Please don't judge me by what you've heard of my past—not everything is black and white." He was tempted to say he that is without sin, cast the first stone, but he suspected that would only rile her.

Analyzing his words, she paused a moment, then nodded her head. "Fair enough. I'll reserve judgment for now."

"That's all I ask." He gave her a friendly grin. "Well, that and a taste of your lasagna—Sage says it's blue-ribbon worthy."

A little while later, Adam and Sage stood outside a waist-high, portable fence, which surrounded the small carousel where Jenna was riding a pink-and-white unicorn. Adam was holding the little girl's balloons—he was the only one she would entrust them to. She was such a sweet kid and would always have a permanent place in his heart, right next to Matthew and Sage.

His mind went over the information Shane had called him with last night. After Adam had contacted his foster brother and filled him in on what had happened, Shane had called in a favor with an FBI buddy who'd made a few discreet inquiries. They hadn't wanted to ruffle any feathers with the local sheriff nor possibly alert Sherman that he was under suspicion. Unfortunately, the rancher had come through squeaky clean. He paid his taxes diligently, and there were no signs of embezzlement or dirty business practices, or anything else for that matter. There hadn't even been any reports of disgruntled employees or business associates or domestic violence complaints. According to all reports, the man was the salt of the earth, but Adam had a hard time believing it. The man wanted Sage's property badly—the questions were why and how far he would go to get it.

Beside him, Sage was talking to two women about some PTA meeting that had gotten everyone in an uproar over a new school curriculum. Over the carnival noises and chatter, he heard someone call his name. Looking around, he saw Matthew and Toby sharing a seat on the Ferris wheel, and they were waving at him as they began a descent from the top of it. In the seat in front of them sat Josh and his father. Adam smiled and waved back at the boys before turning back to check on Jenna.

Barely a minute had passed by before the sound of metal against metal clanged loudly, immediately followed by screams of terror that sent shivers through Adam's spine. One of the loudest cries belonged to Matthew. Adam looked up in horror to see the seat the two boys were in, near the top of the ride, had become partially disconnected from the steel frame of the wheel. Toby's feet were dangling in the air as Matthew tried desperately to keep him from falling while holding onto the chair, which was hanging at a dangerous angle. Beside Adam, Sage shrieked her son's name.

Letting go of the balloons in his hand, Adam pushed through the gasping and screaming crowd. He vaulted the metal divider to where the attendant was frantically pushing buttons on the Ferris wheel's control panel. The young man glanced up, his eyes wide in fear. "It's stuck! It won't move! I can't get them down!"

"Jesus Christ!" Adam's head whipped back and forth, scanning the massive apparatus. The steel spokes of the wheel were connected in a way that he could climb it.

Jumping over another metal divider, he reached up and grabbed hold of the nearest beam, hauling himself up. He looked upward and grabbed the next one, ignoring the horrified crowd below and the crying children, who were still safe in their locked but rocking seats. His attention was on the two screaming boys who were holding on for dear life sixty feet in the air. "Matthew! Toby! Don't move! I'm coming up!"

"Adam! I'm right behind you!" Toby's father, Chris Miller, was a few feet down on the other side of the steel frame, climbing as quickly as he could.

An unknown male voice shouted from below. "Just secure them! The fire department is bringing the bucket!"

The aerial bucket truck would be the easiest way to get them down, but first, Adam and Chris had to reach the boys and keep them from falling. It was doubtful either one would survive the drop from that height, and Adam prayed as he'd never prayed before.

Hand over hand, the two men scaled the structure.

Adam blocked out everything but which beam he needed to grab next and the two boys swinging precariously. The disabled seat was squeaking as it hung down from one side. The fear in their eyes kicked him in the gut.

Dear God, please don't let us fail.

The roar of the fire engine came to a stop far below them, and the brakes released a loud *swoosh* as the air was compressed from them. Adam was about five feet from where Toby's sneakers swung back and forth. From here, he could see that Matthew was more stable than his friend and held onto Toby's belt, keeping him from falling. "You're doing good, Matthew. Just hold on. Toby, don't move. I'll come up and grab you, but don't move until I say so, okay?"

"Y-yes . . . h-hurry!"

Chris was now even with Adam, but he had to maneuver to the inside of the frame to reach the boys. "I'm right here, Toby. Do exactly what Adam told you to do."

"O-okay, Dad."

"Good boy."

His heart pounding, Adam brought himself parallel to Toby before moving in behind him and grabbing the boy around the waist. Once Adam had Toby secure, Chris positioned himself so Matthew could let go of his friend without losing his grip on the back of the seat. The weight of both boys was now supported by the men, whose legs were long enough to reach the wheel's spokes beneath them.

Chris glanced down. Now that they had the boys stabilized, his voice sounded more in control. The experienced volunteer fireman in him had replaced the terrified father. "Bucket's on its way up on your side, Adam. They'll bring it as close to you as possible."

Long seconds passed as the extended aerial arm was

raised up. When the bucket stopped behind and a little below Adam, one of the two firemen on board opened the side gate. "If you've got a good grip on the boy, you can take a step back. You've got about a six-inch drop to the floor."

Wrapping his arms tightly around Toby's waist, Adam eyed Matthew and Chris. "Got him?"

The other man tightened his hold. "Yeah, just no sudden movements. Nice and slow."

Taking a deep breath, Adam eased his right foot backward. A hand at his lower back guided him as he brought Toby into the bucket with him. Setting the boy on his feet, he watched as the two firemen reached out and pulled Matthew and then Chris to safety.

The older of the two volunteers spoke into his radio. "All secure. Coming down."

The crowd below them erupted into cheers as Toby threw his arms around his father, and a trembling Matthew did the same to Adam. The fire department would have to retrieve the people from the other stranded cars, one by one, but compared to this part of the rescue, that would be a piece of cake.

When the arm was completely folded again, Adam, Chris, and the boys scrambled down from the bucket onto the ground. Sage and Ashley rushed to their sons, crying and embracing them as hard as possible. Adam glanced around and saw Evan standing next to Maddie, who was holding Jenna. Tears streamed down the little girl's face, and he strode over to take her in his arms. "It's all right, Little Bird. Matthew's safe."

"You thave . . . thaved him, just like you thaved Ruby Tuethday." Her arms went around his neck, and she buried her face in his throat.

As the volunteers worked quickly to get the rest of the

riders off the disabled Ferris wheel, people were clapping Adam and Chris on the back, commending their bravery and swiftness and congratulating them on a successful rescue. Adam set Jenna down, and she ran to hug her brother and mother. It was a tearful but happy reunion.

When Ashley finally released her son, she spun around, zeroed in on Adam, and threw her arms around him. "I don't know how I'll ever be able to repay you. Thank you so much, Adam. I-I could have lost Toby." She began to sob.

He smiled and patted her back. "*Shh*. It's okay, Ashley. They're safe and unharmed."

Pulling back so she could look him in the face, her teary, apologetic gaze met his understanding one. "I'm so sorry I judged you—it was unfair of me." The corners of her mouth ticked up in a grin. "I'm going to make you a lasagna a week for the next six months."

Throwing his head back, he let out a hearty chortle, happy to have a release for the gut-wrenching tension still flowing through him. His legs were now shaking from the adrenaline overload and didn't seem to want to stop anytime soon. "Not necessary, but who am I to turn down an awesome lasagna? Make me one next week, and we'll call it even."

"Deal!"

As the woman turned back to her husband and son, Sage took her place. "Thank you, Adam."

She hugged him, and unlike his body's non-response to Ashley, he felt himself grow hard, and his breath caught as he inhaled the scent of her citrus shampoo. His arms went around her waist, and for a brief moment, he held her flush against him. There was no hiding his cock's reaction to her nor her hardened nipples, which he felt through both their thin T-shirts. Sage gave him a final squeeze before pulling away. A sexy blush now stained her pale cheeks, and her gaze was pinned to his chest. "I-I think we better go home. That was more than enough excitement for the day. Heck, for an entire lifetime."

"No arguments here, but I better replace Jenna's balloons on the way back to the car before she realizes they're missing."

With a shaky laugh, Sage hugged him again. "Sounds like a plan."

Chapter Twelve

Singing along to Miranda Lambert on the radio, Sage drove the speed limit as she left town. It was twenty minutes before midnight on Saturday night, and even though she'd only had two glasses of wine over several hours, she had to watch for any deer or coyotes, which were famous among the locals for darting out into the road late at night. There were numerous other wild animals in the wooded area, which started at the edge of town and extended for almost three miles before reopening to farm-land. Then again, it wasn't unheard of for someone to come across some cows, sheep, or even a horse in the middle of the road.

The evening had been fun for Sage, with Ashley, Sarah, and Jess all getting together for a girl's night out, some-thing the four friends hadn't done in a while. Ashley and Jess had birthdays coming up during the week, so they'd gone to the only real honky-tonk they had in Rosewood. While there was a bar at the American Legion post and another at a little hole-in-the-wall that was simply called The Tavern, the Sip & Dip had a large dance floor and live music on two Saturdays of the month. Instead of booths, picnic tables were used throughout the establishment, and the floor was covered with sawdust and peanut shells. One of the girls' favorite local bands, Playing Possum, had been there tonight, and they'd all danced up a storm.

Sage had almost begged off—after last week's nightmare with the Ferris wheel, she'd been having difficulty letting either of her children out of her sight. Matthew had recovered from the frightening ordeal, and so had Toby, but Sage thought it would be a very long time before either boy dared go on another amusement ride. And that was fine with her.

While she'd enjoyed being out with her girlfriends, a huge part of Sage missed sitting on the back porch after dinner with Adam, talking about anything and everything. They'd fallen into a routine, and it was one she felt comfortable with. With school out, the kids were allowed to stay up later, so everyone converged on the porch, where the adults enjoyed their evening coffee. Sage and Maddie would chat while working on their knitting. They were part of a group that knitted blankets for premature babies or cancer patients who were undergoing treatment at the county hospital. Sage wasn't as fast as Maddie, who had taught her how to knit, but at least her finished pieces were on par with her mentor's. Meanwhile, Evan and Adam would continue with their current chess game. The men were evenly matched, and each game lasted about a week before they set up for a new one.

Sometimes the kids would have friends over, or they'd spend the night at a sleepover. Other times, they'd find something to do together. Matthew loved bringing out the telescope Mark had given him a few months before he died. Sage had gotten him a bunch of books on astronomy, and he loved finding the constellations in the sky. Jenna usually played nearby with her dolls and other toys or sometimes sat in Adam's lap while he studied the chessboard.

Then long after the children had gone to bed and the older couple retired to their own cottage, Sage and Adam would either steal away to his bedroom to make love or stay out under the stars just talking. She hadn't realized how much she missed having a man to talk to. Sometimes a woman needed her girlfriends, sometimes her parents or siblings, but other times, having a man listen to her . . . really listen to her about her fears and dreams, was what she needed. Sage had been lucky to find another companion to fill the hole in her heart caused by Mark's death. But for how long?

Somehow, someway, Adam had become part of their little family, but she was still afraid to ask him what his long-term plans were. She couldn't decide which would be worse, knowing he'd eventually be leaving or having it come as a surprise one day. Of course, another option was that he would stay, and things would continue as they had been recently. A final possibility was that one of these days, he'd tell her he'd fallen madly in love with her, as she had with him, and he wanted to make an honest woman out of her. She just wished she knew where she stood with him.

Sage's headlights flashed on a blur, and she slammed on the brakes as a three-point buck leaped past the hood of her truck. The back end of the truck swung wide, and she yanked the steering wheel to the right and then left, trying to maintain control. The truck corrected itself and finally came to a stop.

Her heart pounded, and Sage gasped for air, not realizing she'd been holding her breath. "Holy shit!"

Glancing over her shoulder, she saw the buck was long

gone. Sage had missed the deer's hind legs by inches. A full minute ticked by before her hands eased from their death grip on the steering wheel, and she lifted her foot from the brake and eased the accelerator down. Her heart rate slowly returned to normal as she drove ten miles below the speed limit for the next two miles. By the time she reached the far end of the woods and the beginning of Davidson's farm, with its acres and acres of fresh vegetables growing in the Oklahoma soil, she'd almost recovered completely and sped up a little more.

Three miles later, she made the right turn onto the long, dirt driveway of Heaven's Pastures Ranch. With all the recent rain they'd had, there were plenty of new potholes for the tires to hit, and the truck rocked back and forth as she drove over them as slowly as possible. The last thing she needed was to bottom out and put a hole in the oil pan. It would cost money to have someone repair it with new fill.

That had been another reason she'd gone out tonight. Bart Sherman had been over again with another offer to buy her property. Why the man was so insistent, she didn't know, but it would be a cold day in hell before she sold the ranch that had been in her husband's family for generations. Somehow, someway, she'd find a way to make it a success. At least, once the first two foals were sold next week, she'd be able to catch up on her mortgage. Then when the others were sold, she could take care of a few additional things that needed financial attention.

As she approached the house, she noticed the light in the living room was on, but the front porch light was out. That was strange. She'd left it on when she'd gone out earlier, and Adam had no reason to turn it off. In fact, he'd said he would leave it on for her. Maybe the bulb blew.

Before she could pull into the spot where she usually parked, the headlights lit up the porch, and Sage noticed something else was wrong. Stopping the truck in its tracks, she squinted while trying to figure out what the shadowy figure was on the welcome mat. It took her a moment to realize it was Benji. But why was he just lying there and not rushing to greet her?

Turning off the engine but leaving the headlights on to see what was wrong with the dog, Sage grabbed her purse and opened the driver's door. Climbing down, she softly called out, "Benji? What's wrong, boy?"

Sage took one, maybe two, steps before a massive hand came from behind and slapped over her mouth, pulling her back hard against a brick wall of a body and causing her to drop her purse. Her heart jumped to her throat as another hand came around and flashed a knife in her face. The huge blade glinted in the moonlight, and she struggled in vain to get free or scream until a hot, alcohol-laced breath brushed over her ear and cheek, and a man growled, "Quiet or I'll break the door down and kill those brats of yours."

❤

MATTHEW FLIPPED OVER ONTO HIS SIDE, TRYING TO FIND A comfortable spot so he could go back to sleep, but a light shining through the edges of the window shade fell right on his face. Blinking, he rubbed his eyes and sat up a little. He pushed the shade to the side, and the bright light intensified. As his pupils adjusted, he saw it was the headlights from his mom's truck. She must have just pulled in and was still listening to a song she loved on the radio. She did that often, sitting in the driver's seat with the doors shut, singing along with the music until the song ended. He always pretended it embarrassed him, but deep down, he loved it. It reminded him of when she would sing him to sleep before he grew too old for nursery rhymes. Occasionally, he'd stand outside Jenna's door at night while Mom put his sister to bed and listen as she sang.

Letting the shade fall, he was about to lie back down when something odd clicked in his brain. Taking another peek out the window, he tried to figure out what seemed off about the vehicle, and then it hit him. The driver's door was wide open. He waited a moment, expecting his mom to climb out of the truck at any second, but she didn't. Maybe she was sick or hurt. Unsure, Matthew stared at the truck, willing his mother to appear. Almost a full minute passed without any signs of her, and his worry got the best of him.

Flipping the covers off, he stood and padded barefoot across the room. Opening the door, he paused to listen, but the only thing he heard was the ticking of the old cuckoo clock on the hallway wall. The lights were off in his mom's room, but with the moonlight, he could tell she wasn't in there. Across the hall, Jenna was sound asleep in her bed, her small night light illuminating her face. She always slept with the door open a few inches, and he crept past in silence, not wanting to wake her.

One of the lamps in the living room was on, giving him enough light to see where he was going. When he reached the foyer, he began to have second thoughts. Adam had been watching TV with them earlier, but after both kids had gone to bed and fallen asleep, he'd returned to his cottage, which was only about fifty feet from the main house.

Maybe I should get him, Matthew thought, but then

scrapped the idea. He was old enough to check on his mom alone, even though his body was quivering for some unknown reason.

Flipping the two locks on the door, he pulled it open and almost tripped over Benji. The dog was sleeping on the welcome mat. Or was he?

"Benji?" Matthew squatted down and stroked the animal's furry side. He was breathing but didn't wake up. Matthew shook him a little as fear of the unknown swirled throughout his young body. "Benji, wake up."

When the dog still didn't respond, Matthew stood and stepped over him, his eyes on the truck in the driveway. There was no sign of his mom. Something was wrong . . . something was very wrong. Scared of what he might find if he investigated, he knew what he had to do.

Spinning back around, he rushed through the house and out the backdoor. Ignoring the pebbles and dirt under his feet, he sprinted to the cottage, and the man who he hoped would tell him everything was all right, that it was just a nightmare he'd wake up from.

Please, let everything be all right!

———— ♥ ————

ADAM'S EYES GREW HEAVY AS THE WORDS ON THE PAGE BLURRED together. A yawn escaped him as he marked his place in the book he was reading. He wished he could stay awake since he'd told Sage she could join him in bed when she got home, but it was getting late, and he couldn't keep his eyes open any longer. He was glad she was out having fun with her friends.

Setting the book on the nightstand, he reached up to shut off the light but froze when someone pounded hard on his door.

"Adam! Adam! Help!"

Throwing the covers off at Matthew's frantic voice, he rushed to the door in nothing but his shorts and yanked it open. Barefoot, the young boy was almost in tears, and Adam's gut clenched. "What's wrong?"

"I-I don't know. Benji won't—won't wake up, and M-Mom—"

Panic assailed him as he grabbed Matthew's shoulders, yet he tried to speak calmly. "What about your mom?"

"I-I don't know," he repeated. "Her tr-truck is in the drive-driveway, b-but I don't think s-she's in it, and Benji won't wake up on the porch."

Oh God! Running back to his bedroom, he threw on the clothes he'd taken off earlier and shoved his feet into his Timberline work boots without socks on, not bothering to tie the loose laces. Returning to Matthew, he followed the boy to the main house, through the kitchen, and out to the foyer. The front door was still open, and Benji was lying on his side, his breathing slow but noticeable. Unable to formulate a thought about what had happened to the dog, Adam stepped over him and hurried to the truck with its headlights still burning bright. "Sage?"

Rounding the hood, he found the driver's door wide open and Sage missing. Her purse was on the ground with its contents spilled out around it. Adam's panic turned into terror. He spun around once, then twice, searching for her even though he knew she was gone. "Sage!"

His desperate shout was met with the sound of crickets singing in the night. His gaze went to the ground, and he spotted Sage's cell phone and truck keys among the scattered items. Snatching them up, he dialed 9-1-1 on the phone as he ran back inside past Matthew, who looked so confused and was trying not to cry. Adam would comfort the boy in a minute, but first, he needed help.

"9-1-1, what is your emergency?" At least the male dispatcher didn't sound as bored as the one from the day Adam had been shot at.

"This is Adam Westfield at Heaven's Pasture Ranch," he announced with a calm he didn't feel as he picked up the cordless phone from the living room and handed it to Matthew. "Call Evan, Matthew, and tell him to hurry over here."

After making sure his order was being followed, Adam returned his attention to the dispatcher. "Sage Hammond is missing, and I think she's been kidnapped. Her truck is in the driveway, door wide open, lights on, and her purse has been dumped on the ground. Our dog is on the porch, unconscious but breathing. I think he may have been poisoned. I need the sheriff and deputies out here immediately."

"Stay on the line, Mr. Westfield, while I dispatch the radio cars. Then I'll need more information."

Adam paced back and forth for what seemed like an eternity. After finishing his call to Evan, Matthew knelt beside Benji and stroked the animal's side. Adam crossed the foyer and placed a hand on the top of the boy's head, trying to silently reassure him. It was only then he realized the porch light was off. Reaching over, he found the switch was up as it should be. He flipped it down and then back up with no response. Stepping out onto the porch again, he inspected the light and found the bulb was completely missing. Whoever was responsible for Sage's disappearance had apparently thought of everything.

Once Evan and Maddie arrived, Adam would leave the children in the older woman's care and have Evan transport Benji to the 24-hour veterinarian hospital a few miles away. He'd then take Sage's vehicle and go question suspect number one on his very short list of people who had an axe to grind with her.

The dispatcher came back on the line with a litany of questions, such as where Sage had gone this evening, with whom, and what time did Adam think she may have gotten home before disappearing. He also asked for a description of what Sage had been wearing tonight. As Adam answered each question, his desperation grew. He wanted to jump into the truck and find her, but he couldn't leave the kids alone.

Just as the dispatcher once again said that help was coming, Evan and Maddie burst through the backdoor. Disconnecting the call, Adam gave the couple a complete but brief rundown of what had happened. Maddie retrieved a blanket from the hall closet and helped Evan and Matthew get Benji loaded into the older man's truck after he'd pulled it around from where he'd parked it behind the house.

Meanwhile, Adam snatched Mark's old rifle from its perch over the fireplace and found a box of ammo that Sage had told him was in her dresser drawer. He had to get out of there before the sheriff's deputies pulled up and prevented him from leaving. Rushing through the front door, he pulled up short when Evan held up a hand to stop him. The man reached into his vehicle, retrieved his Glock 9mm handgun, and swapped it out with the rifle Adam was carrying. "Easier to conceal. Just make sure it's justifiable, son. I'll call you as soon as I drop Benji off."

Adam checked the weapon's magazine and saw it was

fully loaded. It had been a long time since he'd shot one of Harry's weapons at the shooting range the cop had belonged to, but some things were like riding a bike. After giving Maddie and Matthew a reassuring nod, he hurried over to Sage's truck, climbed into the driver's seat, started the engine, and put the vehicle in drive before he'd even gotten the door shut. He knew he was probably disturbing evidence, but saving Sage before something horrible happened to her was more important. He just hoped he found her in time.

Chapter Thirteen

At the end of the drive, Adam turned right and floored the accelerator. In the rearview mirror, he could see the lights of several patrol cars on their way to Heaven's Pasture. Maddie would give them what little information there was, but Adam couldn't wait for the whole initial report to be taken before anything was done. His heart threatened to beat out of his chest as he pushed the truck far past the 35 M.P.H. speed limit, then slammed on the brakes as the turnoff he was looking for approached rapidly. Sharply turning the wheel, he almost lost control as the tail of the truck swerved wide, but then the wheels recovered and found traction again.

Bart Sherman's two-story ranch house came into view, along with a large bunkhouse and several barns. Very few lights were on in any of the buildings, but Adam didn't care who he was about to wake up. Skidding to a stop in front of the main house, he grabbed the gun and leaped from the truck, leaving it running. He stormed up the stairs and pounded on the door. "Sherman! Open up! Where is she? Sherman!"

He was about to rear back and attempt to kick the door in, but interior lights came on, and through the long narrow window next to the door, he saw the ranch owner descending the stairs. Adam slammed his fist against the door, his impatience and fear combining within him. "Open the damn door!"

It swung open, and Adam wasted no time grabbing the other man by his shirt and throwing him up against the wall in the foyer. He pressed the weapon to Sherman's temple, and the man's eyes went wide with fear as an uncontrollable rage came over Adam. "Where is she, you son-of-a-bitch?"

"W-where's who? What the hell do you think you're doing, Westfield? Are you out of your fucking mind?"

Adam pressed his hand harder into Sherman's chest. "Sage! Where is she? What did you do to her?"

"Bart! Oh, my God! Let him go!" The shrieking female voice penetrated Adam's mind, and he glanced up the stairs to see Helen Sherman standing there in her bathrobe. She was pale, and her eyes were filled with the same terror Adam was feeling but for a different reason—mainly the loaded gun being pointed at her husband's head.

Adam released the man and took a step back, trying to get himself under control. He wasn't any good to Sage if he couldn't think straight. "Sage has been kidnapped."

"What?" Sherman responded in disbelief. "What the hell are you talking about?"

"Sage's truck was left in her driveway, headlights on, door wide open. Everything from her purse was on the ground, and I'm not sure, but I think the dog was poisoned."

"And you think I had something to do with it? You're

crazy!" Sherman took a deep breath and ran his hand down his face. When he spoke again, he was much calmer. "Listen, Westfield, I may want Sage's land, but legally. I would never hurt her or anyone else. I've been here all night with Helen."

Adam's mind raced, but he lowered his weapon. "What about your foreman?"

Shaking his head, the man said, "He's down in Dallas on business for me. And I would never ask one of my men to do something like this. I'd be the first one to make sure they were locked up if they did do it."

None of this made any sense. Adam had been sure Sherman was involved in Sage's disappearance, but when he looked at him again, finally noticing the man's pajama pants and white T-shirt, and then at Helen, he knew he was barking up the wrong tree. *Shit.*

"Okay, if it's not you or one of your men, then . . ." Then he had no clue who had her and where she might be. His terror returned.

"Did you call the sheriff's department?"

"Yeah, they sent patrol cars to the ranch, but I didn't wait for them. Maddie is there with the kids, and Evan took the dog to the vet." He paced back and forth in the small foyer, racking his brains for anyone else who might want to harm Sage. What if it was a random crime? What if, by the time they found her, it was too late?

"Listen . . ." Sherman stepped in front of him and set a hand on his shoulder. A fatherly expression was on his face, one filled with concern and understanding. "I meant what I said. Sage is a nice woman, and the last thing I want to see is her hurt in any way. Let me throw on some clothes and get my men, and we'll help you look."

He nodded and released his bottom lip he hadn't realized he'd sunk his teeth into. "Yeah, thanks. But I have no idea where the hell we're supposed to be looking."

"Give me two minutes, and I'll go with you. I know the area like the back of my hand." When Adam nodded again, Sherman strode to the stairs. "Helen, call over to the bunkhouse and rally the men. I want everyone out there looking for Sage."

Less than ten minutes later, Sherman and Adam were sitting side by side in Sage's truck. The older man had sent his ranch hands over to Heaven's Pastures to meet up with the sheriff's deputies and help with whatever search they were planning. But Adam couldn't wait for anyone to make a decision. Even though he had no idea where to start looking, he couldn't sit and twiddle his thumbs. At the very least, he had to drive around looking for her, and maybe something or someone would give them a clue.

"Head toward town. We'll start there and then widen the search," Sherman said as he plugged his cell phone's charger into the port in the dashboard. "In the meantime, I'll get Cosgrove on the line and see if his deputies found anything yet."

Adam nodded silently as he turned left out of the long driveway and onto the main road that would take them past Sage's place and into Rosewood. His jaw was clenched almost as tightly as his hands were on the steering wheel. If anything happened to Sage, he didn't know what he would do. The woman and her children had pulled Adam from the dark and into the light again —something he'd never expected anyone to be able to do. They'd healed him. If any good could have come from Brother Andre's assault of his young victim and subsequent death at Adam's hands, being part of Sage, Matthew, and Jenna's lives and loving each of them was it. Adam belonged with them—he knew it in his soul.

Sage's cell phone rang, but Adam's hopes were dashed when it was just Evan telling him Benji was still alive and the vet was pumping his stomach. Evan was heading back to the ranch to join the search party that was being organized. More deputies had been dispatched, and others were responding from other towns in the county.

When the drive into Rosewood didn't generate results, Sherman instructed Adam to turn around and make a left on Briarcliff Drive on the edge of town. It ran along the east end of the woods and led out to a lake that was a gathering spot for teens during hot summer evenings.

"You really care for her, don't you?"

Adam was startled at the understanding he heard in the other man's voice, but he kept his gaze on the dark road that was only illuminated by the truck's headlights. The moon had disappeared behind some clouds, making the surrounding area appear eerie. If this had been a horror movie, Adam would expect fog to roll in and someone to jump out from behind a tree.

"Yeah, I do. Hell, somewhere along the line, I fell in love with her."

Sherman snorted. "And that surprises you why?"

Good question.

"Because I don't deserve it." Adam wasn't sure why, but he found he couldn't just leave it at that, maybe because he owed the man something for holding a gun on him earlier. "I was in prison for killing a man." His declaration was met by silence, and he continued with the extremely short version of what had happened many years ago. "I never meant for it to happen, but he'd been in the middle of molesting a small boy. My rage took over, and the next thing I knew, I'd thrown him across the room, and his head hit a wooden chest hard enough to kill him."

"And you went to prison for saving the boy? I would've thought they'd have given you a medal." The incredulous tone was hard to miss.

"I wouldn't let the boy testify. I took my punishment and did my time."

Aside from the sounds from the motor and tires, silence filled the truck's cab. Seconds ticked by as the other man digested what he'd been told.

"Why'd you tell me? You could have just let me go on thinking the worst of you."

Adam took a deep breath and let it out. "Because if Sage will have me, I plan on being around for a very long time. I'd rather not have an enemy as my neighbor. I'm sorry I pulled the gun on you."

Bart snorted. "A man in love will do anything when his woman is in danger. I would have done the same thing had the situation been reversed."

Adam was about to glance over at the man, but something ran into the road, and he slammed on the brakes. Yanking the steering wheel to the left, he lost control of the vehicle, and it careened off the pavement. Every muscle in Adam's body seized, and with a bone-crushing impact, the truck went head-first into a tree.

———— ❤ ————

CRAMPED IN THE TRUNK OF SETH CHAPMAN'S BEAT-UP, FIFTEEN-year-old Pontiac Bonneville, Sage tried to turn over so she'd be facing the back of the vehicle, but with a spare tire and other junk, it was difficult to maneuver. She'd been terrified when he'd threatened her children and let herself be led on foot back toward the main road, waiting for an opportunity to run—or kick him in the balls and then run.

When they'd reached where he'd hidden his car, across the road from her property in a small copse of trees, he'd threatened her with the knife to make her climb into the trunk. She'd followed his order because she knew how to escape from one. Mark had shown her a video once on YouTube after hearing a woman in California had saved herself from a kidnapper who had locked her in the trunk of her own car. If Sage could flip over, she'd be able to do exactly what she'd seen in the demonstration a reporter and police officer had put together. What Seth planned on doing with her, she had no idea, but it couldn't be good. He'd already hurt or killed Benji, and no one just kidnapped someone for non-nefarious reasons. Crazy was crazy—no need to analyze it until she escaped.

Country music wailed loudly through the rear seat, so she knew it was useless to yell, even if they were stopped. No one would hear her. The car hit another bump in the road, lifting Sage up until she hit the top of the trunk, then fell again. Almost every inch of her body smarted from the impact. Pushing what felt like tools, cans, plastic bags, and other junk out of her way, she finally managed to turn over. Her eyes had become accustomed to the pitch-black interior, and she quickly spotted the emergency trunk release— it was glowing in the dark, just like in the video.

Pulling the plastic handle, her heart sank when nothing happened. She yanked on it again, and her hand flew upward, smacking the metal above her, the latch still in her hand and now disconnected from whatever it had been attached to. Her knuckles stung like hundreds of angry bees had attacked them, and she knew without looking she'd taken a few layers of skin off them. *Damn it!*

The vehicle turned right, and Sage braced herself using her arms and legs. Panic was setting in, and she inhaled deeply, then coughed violently as the fumes from a combination of stale food, oil, gasoline, and God-knew-what-else invaded her lungs.

Stay calm and find some way to escape.

She had to do everything she could to get back to her children . . . and to Adam. She had to tell all of them how much she loved them and take the risk that Adam might not feel the same way. Somehow, she'd been lucky enough to love two men in her lifetime and damn it, the second man didn't even know it. But Sage would tell him if she ever got out of there.

Another sharp turn and Sage rattled around in the trunk as the vehicle drove over a lot of bumps and potholes. They had to be on a dirt road, but Sage had no idea where. She'd lost her sense of direction and of time not long after being ordered into the trunk before it was shut. If the bastard hadn't held that huge hunting knife so close to her chest, she would have gone on the offensive. But the man was at least eight inches taller than her and outweighed her by a good hundred-and-thirty pounds or so. Her only chance was to surprise him with something that disabled him when he opened the trunk again so that she could run. Maybe even get the keys from him, so she could drive away and leave him wherever they were going. She'd call 9-1-1 as soon as she could.

Feeling around, Sage tried to identify the objects in the trunk, hoping for a crowbar or something she could swing at him. She figured it was too much to ask for Seth to keep a loaded gun back there, but it didn't stop her from praying for one—or a miracle or two.

Seth hit another hard bump, and Sage's head smacked the trunk frame. "*Ow!* Watch the damn potholes, you asshole!" There was no way he'd heard her over Trace Adkins and Blake Shelton's duet blaring over the radio, but it made her feel a little better to vent her anger which was quickly overtaking her panic. Her searching fingers found something hard, metal, and heavy. Grabbing it, she inspected the item with both hands and figured out it was a wrench. She'd be more than happy to throw it at Seth's head when he opened the trunk. That was one weapon. Maybe she could find something else.

After another minute of searching and bouncing around in the confined space, she found what felt like a canister. Shaking it, she heard the distinct sound of a pea banging against the inside of the can. It was a metal, plastic, or glass ball used to mix aerosol paint. *Perfect.* She could spray the paint in his face and hopefully blind him.

Sage removed the plastic top of the canister and located the spray button and nozzle by touch. It would really suck if she sprayed it at her own face. With the paint in her non-dominant hand and the wrench in the other, she was ready to face her abductor, and none too soon. The vehicle slowed and came to a stop.

Her heart pounded in her chest, and she tried to keep her rage in the forefront of her mind. Hesitating could ruin any chance she had of getting away. The engine shut off along with the radio, and the sudden silence was almost as deafening. The driver's door opened, and that side of the car recovered and lifted without the pressure of the heavy man on its abused shocks.

Dirt and pebbles crunched under his boots as he strode

to the back of the car. Sage wanted to take a deep breath to steady her trembling hands, but she couldn't risk another coughing fit. The scrape of metal against metal as he inserted the key into the lock had her tensing. Suddenly the trunk lid lifted, and even though the moon was behind some clouds, Sage could still see well enough to aim. She didn't waste a single second, spraying the paint into Seth's face before he had a chance to do anything.

He roared in anger and pain as his nose, cheeks, eyes, chin, and forehead turned MTN 94 Guacamole Green. Stumbling backward, he tried to wipe the paint off his face with one hand while lashing out into the air with the hunting knife he still held. Unable to throw the wrench at him from the confines of the trunk, Sage dropped the canister and used her hands and feet to scramble out of the car. Once standing, she threw the metal tool directly at Seth's head and was rewarded with a loud thud as it hit him right above his temple before he went down on his knees. Unfortunately, she hadn't knocked him out, and he was still swinging the knife while trying to clear his vision with his other hand. "You bitch! You fucking bitch! I'm going to kill you! Goddamn it!"

Realizing they were in the woods at a dead end on the dirt road, Sage wouldn't be able to turn the car around easily, even if she was able to get hold of the keys, which were on the ground next to Seth's knees. She had no alternative but to run as if her life depended on it. And seeing her kidnapper struggle to stand, it looked like her life *did* depend on it.

Taking off at a full run, Sage headed back up the road they'd come in on. Her cowgirl boots pummeled the gravel beneath them as her heart threatened to beat out of her chest. Behind her, Seth shouted, "Get back here, you bitch!"

The sound of his boots on the ground mingled with hers, and she didn't dare take a glance back. She needed to keep her eyes on what was ahead of her in the dimmed moonlight. Sage thought she was in good physical condition with all the hard work that came with working on a ranch, but her lungs and legs weren't used to sprinting for long distances, and both began to burn.

An "*oomph*" behind her was followed by more cursing. He must have tripped but recovered because she could hear him running again. "Goddamn it, bitch!"

The end of the dirt road was approaching, and Sage racked her brain to remember which direction they turned from. She could swear they'd made a right turn, which meant she had to go left. Gasping for air, she pushed her aching legs harder, but Seth was gaining on her. Without conscious thought, she glanced over her shoulder and saw there was only about ten feet between them. She wasn't going to make it. Even if she made it onto the paved road, he'd be on her before she could get much further.

Sage's foot hit something, causing her to trip and stumble. Her momentum sent her onto the pavement just as headlights rounded a bend. Everything happened so fast, Sage was sure she would be hit and killed, but she was frozen like a deer facing the same fate. A screech of brakes on asphalt had her throwing her hands up in front of her face—as if that would save her—and the truck fishtailed out of control. It missed Sage by inches as it flew off the road and into a tree. The sound of metal crumbling and glass breaking was deafening as the vehicle slammed to a stop, then faded away until the only things she heard were a hissing noise coming from the engine and the hammering of her own heart.

Sage took a few steps to see if whoever was in there was

okay and if they could help her, but a large hand clamped down on her shoulder, and an arm wrapped around her waist, pulling her up short. A scream pierced the night, and it took a moment for her to realize it was coming from her own throat.

Chapter Fourteen

Pain tormented Adam's body—everything hurt, even his toes. Despite the seatbelt holding him in place and the airbags deploying, the bone-jarring impact had been severe enough to cause some injuries. His knees had connected with the dashboard after it was shoved toward him. The left side of his head had struck the window of the driver's door, shattering the glass, and his hands and arms had taken the blunt impact from the steering wheel.

A wave of dizziness overcame him, and he closed his eyes, willing it to go away. While he didn't think anything was broken, he probably had one helluva concussion. Blood dripped from his chin, and reaching up, he traced the trail up his cheek to above his hairline. His hand came away red and sticky.

What happened?

Obviously, there had been an accident, but what had he been doing right before that? Where was he? A moan beside him had him glancing over. Bart Sherman was semi-unconscious but alive and moving a bit. Adam felt the area near his hip and found the release to unclip his seat belt. His gaze darted around the cab's interior, searching for his or Bart's cell phone so he could call 9-1-1, but a scream pierced the air, sending chills down his spine and causing the hair on his neck to stand up. Suddenly, he was alert and oriented.

Sage!

That was why he'd crashed. She'd run out into the middle of the road, and he'd swerved to avoid hitting her.

"Let go of me! Help!"

"Shut up, you bitch!" The deep, threatening, male voice erupted a volcano of fury from within Adam—something he'd only experienced once before in his life and had prayed he never would again. He reached for the gun that had been on the bench seat between him and Bart, but it was gone—probably thrown under the dashboard. He didn't have time to search for it—he had to get to Sage.

"Let go, you asshole!" Her growled order told him she was strong enough to fight for her life at the moment, but for how long would she be able to continue?

Pulling the handle, Adam tried to push the door open, but no matter how hard he tried, it wasn't budging. His only other choice was through the broken window. Gripping the upper frame, he ignored the few shards of glass still stuck under the rubber lining as they dug into his palms and hoisted himself part of the way out. Contorting his body, he pulled his legs through the confined space and half jumped/half fell to the ground. His head spun, and his dinner threatened to come back up as he stood and stumbled forward. Sage's screams and the bastard's bellowing urged him on.

"*Ow!* You fucking bitch!"

"Let! Me! Go!"

Rounding the truck, he saw them in the middle of the

road. Seth Chapman was trying to pick Sage up, but her intense struggle made it difficult. She must have scratched his face with her fingernails because the left side had four angry, red streaks running down his cheek. One of his arms was wrapped around her upper chest while his other hand was at her waist, holding a huge hunting knife.

A crimson haze filled Adam's vision as he used the side of the truck bed to steady himself. "Chapman! Let her go!"

The man paused as if surprised anyone had survived the accident, and it gave Sage the split second she needed. Lifting her leg, she scraped his shin with the hard heel of her boot while, at the same time, tilted her chin down and bit him on his forearm with everything she had. Chapman roared, releasing her and shoving her forward, which forced her jaw to let go of him. Adam's heart leaped into his throat as the man swung the knife wildly in front of him, and Sage tripped, falling to the ground as the blade sliced the air mere inches away from her head.

Without hesitation, Adam lunged at Chapman, tackling him to the pavement—the knife flew from his hand and skittered across the road. While the bastard outweighed him by a good fifty pounds, Adam's muscle memory from years of training in Krav Maga, boxing, and wrestling kicked in. They rolled around, each trying to gain the upper hand. Sweat and blood poured from their bodies. Fists, arms, and knees connected. Chapman snapped his head forward, aiming for the middle of Adam's face, but he saw it coming and shifted his head to the side. Instead of his nose being struck, his chin exploded in pain, fueling his wrath.

Rolling on top of the bigger man, Adam got his hands around his throat and squeezed with all his might. Chapman gasped for air and clawed at Adam's hands and arms to no avail. His eyes bulged as his face flushed.

Capillaries in his sclerae began to burst, making the white around his pupils and irises look bloodshot. His legs kicked out as his struggles weakened, and still, the pressure remained on his neck. Adam couldn't think. He couldn't feel anything but rage.

A female voice yelling his name tickled the edges of his conscious mind, but it was a single gunshot that had him whipping his head up in alarm. Sherman stood next to Sage, the gun in his hand, pointed in the air toward the woods. Blood dripped on his white T-shirt from a laceration on his forehead as he put a supportive arm around Sage and directed his words at Adam. "Let him go, Westfield. It's over. Let the law give him what he deserves. Don't let the devil do this to you again."

Adam's gaze went to Sage's pale face, and he saw understanding in her eyes as she pleaded with him. "Let him go, Adam. I'm okay. We're all okay. Don't do this, please."

Dropping his chin, he stared at the pathetic man beneath him. He was still gasping for air. Adam had been moments away from killing a man for the second time in his life. "No."

He shook his head as he relaxed his grip. Chapman's lungs heaved for oxygen as Adam pushed off him and stood. He glared at the man. "You're not worth it."

Sirens wailed in the distance as Adam staggered toward Sage, who rushed into his arms. Holding her tightly, he glanced at her neighbor, who had his cell phone in one hand and the gun aimed at Chapman, just in case. Sherman gave him a solitary nod, silently telling him he'd done the right thing.

Pulling back from Sage just enough to bring his hands up to cup her chin, Adam inspected her for injuries. She was bruised and scraped up, but nothing time wouldn't heal. His gaze met her tearful but relieved one. "Thank God, you're okay. I don't know what I would've done if something had happened to you. I love you, Sage."

She gasped as tears rolled down her cheeks. "I love you too, Adam." She buried her head into his chest, wrapping her arms around his neck. "I love you too."

LYING IN SAGE'S BED, ADAM HELD HER CLOSE. IT WAS PAST 10:00 a.m., but Sage was still asleep—she needed it after last night. They'd returned home just before dawn after being evaluated at the emergency room, then released to head to the sheriff's department to give their reports. It had been after four in the morning when they'd gotten home, but Maddie and Evan had been waiting up for them. The children had fallen asleep on the couches in the living room but had woken up and had needed reassurance that their mother was okay before going back to bed.

After Maddie and Evan had gone back to their cottage, Sage had taken Adam's hand and silently led him to her bedroom. They'd stripped down to their underwear and crawled into bed. As he'd taken her into his arms, determined never to let her go, she'd finally had the adrenaline meltdown he'd been warned to expect by the E.R. doctor. Not wanting her children to overhear, she'd cried as quietly as she could while Adam stroked her and murmured words of comfort. He'd told her how proud he was of her and how she'd saved herself.

Adam's declaration of love and Sage's subsequent one

rolled over and over in his mind. There had been no hesitation in her response, nor had she seemed surprised he'd said, "I love you," at all.

He'd never imagined he'd be saying those words to a woman, but once he had, he'd known it was true. He was madly, completely in love with Sage. Where they'd go from here, he wasn't sure, but he knew it would be at each other's side. When she was ready, he'd broach the subject of marriage—he wanted nothing more than to make her his wife.

Beside him, Sage stirred, and as she brushed against his groin, he grew hard immediately. Her eyes blinked open, and she snuggled closer to him. "Let me make love to you, Adam, to remind me that I'm alive."

Maddie had assured them they wouldn't be disturbed until they emerged from the bedroom, letting them sleep as long as they needed. Adam was grateful for the woman's take-charge attitude.

Rolling onto his back, Adam pulled Sage on top of him. "Take whatever you need, my love."

The drowsiness fled from her eyes, and she lowered her head to kiss him. Adam reached behind her and, with clumsy fingers, unhooked her bra and slid it down her arms. Cupping her breasts, he tested their weight, then swiped his thumbs over her taut nipples. Sage nipped at his bottom lip and lashed the abused flesh with her tongue.

Her hands touched him all over, driving his desire higher. He loved how she took charge sometimes and was man enough to be comfortable with her doing so. Each time they made love, he learned more and more about her —what she liked, what made her moan his name, and what made her beg.

Tilting her hips, Sage rubbed her wet heat over his erection as she plunged her tongue into his mouth. He met her taste for taste, touch for touch, thrust for thrust. Her mouth left his as she kissed her way to his jaw and down his neck. "Put your hands behind your head, Adam."

"*Mmmm.*" His eyes closed as he did as she'd requested, savoring the sensations coursing through his body as her mouth, tongue, and teeth did wicked things to him. She slowly made her way down his chest, taking her time and brushing her lips against each one of his bruises. Almost half his body was covered in black and blue—more than he'd realized—from the accident and fight which followed. But her tender touch brought him no pain, only a need for more of everything she was doing to him.

Her hands skimmed his sides to his hips, sending a quiver through his muscles. He felt her smile against his abdomen as she hooked her fingers under the waistband of his briefs and tugged them down until his cock sprung free. His hips bucked as her tongue swiped over the tip, the warmth of her mouth making him shiver in anticipation. He forced his eyes open, so he could watch her take him into her mouth. It was more erotic than he could've ever imagined.

Her gaze was on his as her lips closed around him, and he couldn't hold back the groan that escaped him. Unable to resist touching her, he removed his hand from behind his head and brushed her hair to the side so he could see better. The strands felt like silk between his fingers. He swallowed hard as she made love to him with her mouth, taking him deep. Her tongue swirled around the thick stalk, and her teeth grazed against his skin.

A tingle started low in his spine. "I need you, Sage."

With one final swipe, she rose to her knees and straddled him. Leaning over, she opened the nightstand drawer and retrieved a condom from a new box she must have picked up. Taking the latex circle, she rolled it onto him, almost setting him off with her touch. Without removing her underwear, Sage shifted the fabric out of the way and guided him to her wet core. His hands went to her hips as she eased down, impaling herself on him. Her heat engulfed him as she rolled her pelvis against his.

As much as he wanted to drive into her, he let her set the pace. She needed this probably more than he did, and that was saying a lot. Thoughts of how close he'd come to losing her tried to take up residence in his mind, but Sage lifted her hips, the drag of her walls against his hard flesh bringing him back to the here and now.

Together they set a pace that sent them both spiraling toward the heavens. As he thrust up, she tilted her hips and came down. Her head dropped back on her shoulders, her dark hair cascading down her back as her hands cupped her ivory breasts and played with the rosy nipples, but the whole time her gaze was pinned to his. Adam shifted his hand, so his thumb could stroke her clitoris the way she loved. Faster. Harder. Soaring higher and higher. Her walls began to ripple around him, and she gasped, then keened, as the orgasm hit her. Having her come undone in his arms was the most beautiful thing he'd ever seen. Wanting to watch every second of it, he tried to stave off his own impending release, but the pleasure was far too intense, and with a final thrust, he tumbled into the abyss after her. His eyelids slammed shut as the mind-boggling pleasure coursed through him.

His chest heaved as his lungs took in gulps of oxygen. Sage stilled, then dropped down on her hands on either side of his head as she also tried to catch her breath. He was still deep within her, and neither one moved, trying to keep the intimate connection as long as possible.

Adam ran his calloused hands up and down the silky skin of her arms. "Are you okay?"

Leaning down, she kissed him. "I will be as long as you never let me go."

The corners of his mouth ticked up in a grin. "Well, I guess that means you're going to be just fine because I don't think I'd ever be able to let you go . . . not without ripping out my heart and giving it to you to take with you. I love you, Sage. You're the light of my life that has been missing all these years."

"And I love you, Adam." She gently cupped his whiskered cheek. "I never thought I'd say those words to another man after Mark died. But then you walked into my life at a time when I needed you the most. I don't know if it was divine intervention or not, but I'll thank God every day for sending you to me."

She kissed him again. They knew they had to get up soon, but for a little while longer, they enjoyed each other and professed their love again. Adam couldn't fathom what he'd done to deserve the woman in his arms, but he knew he would never take her nor her love for granted.

Chapter Fifteen

S age enjoyed the rocking motion as Topaz walked up
the path through the trees leading to the pond. Her
arms were wrapped around Jenna's torso as the horse
carried them both. Behind them, Matthew was Othello's
lone rider. While Adam and Evan were handling a new
delivery of hay bales and feed, Sage had decided to spend
some time with just her children. They'd be starting school
again next week, so their afternoons and weekends would
once again be filled with homework, projects, Brownie
troop activities for Jenna, and soccer practice and games for
Matthew. Now that the Little League season was over, a
new sport had been added to the schedule, and he enjoyed
this one much more than the last.

It had been just a week since Sage had been kidnapped,
and she was still sleeping with the light on in her
bedroom's attached bath. Pitch darkness reminded her of
being in the trunk of Seth's car, and she found herself
listening for even the slightest of sounds when the lights
went out. Thankfully, Adam was very understanding and
had been there each time she awoke from a nightmare

flashing back to her ordeal. Having recovered from the hamburger with poison in it, Benji had also been keeping a close eye on Sage since coming home from the veterinary hospital a few days ago. He would whine if her bedroom door was completely shut at night.

After Seth had been hauled away by the sheriff's deputies, Sage, Adam, and Bart were transported to the hospital for examinations. Both men had been diagnosed with minor concussions. Bart had required stitches to his forehead, and Sage's scraped-up arms and hands had to be thoroughly cleaned, but other than that, the three of them had only suffered mild cuts and contusions.

Once they'd given their statements, Bart had one of his men drive Sage and Adam to Heaven's Pastures since her truck had basically been totaled, while another of his employees had given him a lift home. It had been another thirty minutes after that before Sage and Adam had calmed Jenna and Matthew down enough that the children were finally able to go back to bed. On their way out to return to their cottage, Evan and Maddie had told them to sleep in the next day as the older couple would take care of the animals and children.

With everything that had happened and their declarations of love to each other, Sage and Adam had given up all pretense that they weren't a couple. He'd slept in her bed that night, holding her as if he never wanted to let her go, and every night since. Maddie, Evan, Matthew, and Jenna had given them their blessing. Even Ashley had been happy for Sage when she'd stopped by the next afternoon, after learning about the kidnapping and arrest, to make sure her best friend was really okay.

Just as Ashley was leaving, Sheriff Cosgrove had pulled up to the ranch to update them. Seth had given a signed confession about how he'd set fire to the barn, fired the shots at Adam, poisoned Benji, and kidnapped Sage because he claimed to be in love with her. Obsessed with her was more like it. While he'd asked her out several times, no one had any idea how far the man would go to make her his. He'd meant to step in and help her pay for the new barn, but Adam had beaten him to it. Then when Sage had introduced Adam to him as her new boyfriend, as well as her new ranch hand, Seth had decided to try to eliminate the competition. He figured if he wormed his way into her life, he could convince her they belonged together.

A shiver went down Sage's spine. As much as she hated Seth for what he'd put her through, she felt bad for his children and his ex-wife. This would fuel the gossip that took place in Rosewood, and it would be a long time before the whispers and finger-pointing stopped for them.

Dismounting when they reached the small lake, Sage took the two saddlebags that contained their lunches and a few other items and set about preparing their little picnic. Jenna was flitting about, gathering wildflowers for the mason jar her mother always packed when they did this, while Matthew led the horses to the water's edge so they could drink. After securing their leads to a small tree, he unhooked his fishing pole and tackle box from Othello.

For the next hour, Sage let the comfort she found in this place soothe her mind. She'd brought a book and leaned against a tree to read while Jenna and Matthew played. After getting no bites from the fish, Matthew had given up and started up a game of hide-and-seek with Jenna. Sage smiled at them. "Don't go too far when you hide."

"We won't. Safety first," Jenna replied, using the warning Mark had always given them when teaching them something new. Her front tooth was coming in, and over the past few days, her lisp had disappeared.

Sighing, Sage lost herself in the romance/suspense novel she was reading.

". . . nineteen . . . twenty," Matthew called out from where he'd been covering his eyes while Jenna found a place to hide. "Ready or not, here I come!"

Glancing up, Sage scanned the surrounding area. Jenna must have found a good spot because she was nowhere in sight as her brother searched for her. Sage was about to return to her book when a shriek pierced the air. Terror gripped her as she leaped to her feet. "Jenna! Where are you? Jenna!"

"Help, Mommy!" Her voice sounded far away with a slight echo.

"Jenna! Where are you?" Sage and Matthew ran in the direction of the little girl's screams. It took a moment to zero in on where they were coming from, about fifty yards north of the pond, where the trees and brush were thicker as the terrain sloped upward again.

Pushing the dense foliage out of the way, Sage found a rock formation with a hole big enough for her daughter to crawl through but entirely too small for Sage or even Matthew to fit. "Jenna! Are you hurt?"

"N-no, but I can't s-see! It's too dark! I fell! Mommy, get me out!"

Trying to move the rocks by herself was futile, even when she pushed and pulled with all her might. They were huge and embedded deep in the soil. Beside her, Matthew tried to help, but it was no use. Pulling her cell phone from the pocket of her jeans, she held back a curse when she saw there was no reception in this spot. Struggling not to show him how scared she was, Sage grabbed her son's arm.

"Matthew, I need you to ride back to the house and get Adam and Evan. Can you do that for me?"

His big hazel eyes, so much like her own, were filled with fear, but he nodded his head. "I-I think so. Is Jenna going to be all right?"

"She's going to be fine." *Lord, please let that be the truth.* "Tell them what happened. They'll need some tools to make the hole bigger and some rope." Glancing over her shoulder, she eyed the horses. Running over to them, she flipped Othello's reins over the horse's head as Matthew pulled himself up into the saddle. Before letting him go, Sage dug into the saddlebag and found the flashlight they always kept there. "Now hurry, but be careful. Okay?"

"Okay, Mom. I'll bring them back right away. Everything will be all right. We'll get Jenna out of there." Suddenly, her young son appeared ten years older and ready to slay dragons to save his sister.

"Mommy!"

"I'm coming, Jenna!" Returning to the mouth of the cave Jenna had fallen into, Sage watched as Matthew and Othello made their way to the other side of the lake toward the path leading back to the ranch. Squatting down, she shined the flashlight beam into the hole and prayed there weren't snakes or anything else in there with Jenna. "Can you see the light, honey?"

"Yes. Come get me!"

"Matthew went to get help. We'll get you out as soon as we can. Can you come closer to the opening?"

"No! It's too high."

Sage tried pushing and pulling various rocks, but she couldn't move them at all. They varied in size, and between the dirt they were in and the heavier rocks on top, she needed something to create a fulcrum for leverage.

179

Scanning the surrounding area, she spotted a fallen tree limb a few feet away. After placing the flashlight on the ground so it continued to shine into the cave's darkness, she retrieved the thick branch, dragging it back to the rocks. She tried wedging it into several cracks before she found one that was a little wider than the others. Using all her strength, she pushed down on the branch, but the rocks wouldn't budge.

"Mommy! Are you still there!"

"Yes, baby. I'm trying to make the hole bigger, but I think I have to wait for Adam and Evan."

The scared little girl began sobbing, and Sage's heart broke for her. She felt helpless. Sitting by the entrance, she began to sing *Return to Pooh Corner*. It was the same song she used to sing to Jenna when she was an infant to get her to go to sleep after the two a.m. feedings. Sage had grown up loving all things Winnie the Pooh, passing it down to her children.

Jenna's crying eased, and she began to sing along to the Kenny Loggins tribute to the silly old bear. When they finished that one, Sage started another of Jenna's favorite tunes. She wasn't sure how much time had passed, but by the middle of the fifth or sixth song, the rumbling sound of the ATV Evan used around the ranch broke through the forest. A few moments later, it appeared with Adam driving it and Matthew sitting behind him, holding on tight. Steering around to where she was waving him down, he got the vehicle as close as possible before stopping at a downed tree. He killed the engine as Evan appeared on Othello, coming off the path.

Leaning down, she tried to reassure Jenna. "Honey, Adam and Evan are here. We're going to get you out."

"Hurry!"

———— ❤ ————

ADAM RUSHED OVER AND KNELT BESIDE SAGE, ASSESSING THE situation. His pounding heart had slowed a little after seeing Sage was worried but calm. They'd all been through hell these past few months, and he wasn't sure they could handle another life-threatening event. He eyed the entrance to the underground cave. "How the heck did she get in there?" Not waiting for an answer, he raised his voice. "Hey, Little Bird, how's my girl doing?"

"I-I'm scared, Adam."

"There's nothing to be scared of, sweetheart. We're going to get you out in a jiffy. I'm going to drop a light down—step back a little so I don't hit you with it." Turning on the larger, heavy-duty flashlight he'd brought with him, he reached into the hole and let it fall to the frightened girl. "Pick that up and look around. You'll hear a lot of loud noises, but it's just us making the hole bigger. Can you back up away from the hole so nothing falls on you?"

"Uh-huh! It's big down here. There's water down here too."

"Must be part of the underground spring that feeds the pond," Adam told Sage before turning his attention back to Jenna. "Honey, are you standing in the water, or is it dry where you are?"

"It's dry . . . sort of. It's muddy."

"Okay. Stand away from the hole but out of the water."

"Okay, Adam. I'm doing it."

He chuckled at the matter-of-fact tone of voice she was now using. Behind him, Evan and Matthew brought over the tools they would need. A sledgehammer, two pickaxes, a crowbar, and a long length of rope would hopefully be all they needed to get Jenna out of there. "Little Bird, don't look up. There might be dirt and small pieces of rock coming down, and I don't want them to get in your eyes."

"Okay."

Taking the pickaxe Evan handed him, he made sure Sage and Matthew stood far enough away before he hoisted the tool in the air, then swung it at the rocks surrounding the hole. Evan stood opposite him and did the same thing. They alternated their assault, and slowly the larger rocks broke up into smaller ones. It took about twenty minutes, using all the tools in their arsenal, to make the hole big enough for Adam to crawl through. Covered in sweat, he guzzled the bottle of water Sage handed him as Evan wrapped the rope around the trunk of a nearby tree. Evan then attached the rope to a winch on the ATV and took up the slack to lower Adam into the hole.

After tying the other end of the rope around his chest, under his arms, Adam sat at the edge of the hole and let his feet dangle in. "How're you doing, Jenna? I'm coming down, but stay where you are until I get there, okay?"

"Okay, Adam."

Evan started the winch, giving Adam enough slack to ease the rest of his body into the hole. He held on tightly to the rope as he was slowly lowered to the cave's floor. When his feet touched the ground, he glanced up. Sage was looking down at him from an estimated height of nine or ten feet.

He pivoted while untying the rope and saw Jenna standing a few feet away against a rock wall, holding the flashlight. "Come here, Little Bird." Running to him, she threw her arms around his neck when he bent down to pick her up. "Are you okay?"

"Uh-huh."

Taking the flashlight from her, he used the beam to inspect the cave's interior. It was much bigger than he'd expected and went further back into the hill above the pond. As the light caressed the bedrock on the other side of a large puddle of water, something that appeared manmade caught his eye. He couldn't tell what it was since the wall curved around into what looked like a little alcove.

Putting Jenna down, he said, "Stay here a second, sweetheart. I'll be right back."

From above, Sage asked, "What is it, Adam?"

"I don't know. There's something down here. Hang on."

Adam walked along the soft, muddy bank, staying close to the walls so he didn't step in the water. He couldn't tell how deep it was and didn't want to find out the hard way. Any noise he made echoed off the rock. When he reached the alcove, he flashed the light beam into it. "What the . . .?"

There were five boxes, three wooden and two steel, filling the approximately 5'x5' area. From the amount of dirt and mold on them, they'd been there for a very long time. The wood was rotted, and as he tugged on one of the lids, it practically disintegrated under his fingers. The flash-light beam glinted off the contents, and Adam blinked several times because he couldn't believe what he saw. It was mind-boggling.

Jenna repeated her mother's earlier question, "What is it, Adam?"

With a grin, he glanced over his shoulder at her. "I think you found a buried treasure, Little Bird."

Chapter Sixteen

Sage was still in shock as she stared at the pile of silver bullion and the two steel boxes filled with Civil War–era gold coins in the bank's large vault. After getting Jenna and Adam out of the cave yesterday, she'd thought he was crazy when he'd told her and Evan what was down there. But when he'd pulled a large silver bar from the back waistband of his jeans, her mouth had gaped, and she'd been at a loss for words.

Using downed tree limbs and some small bushes, they'd covered the spot up until they could make some phone calls. When they'd reached the house, the first call Adam had Sage make was to her lawyer. Robert Taft had been the Hammond's family attorney since Mark had been a little boy, and Sage trusted him. He'd rushed over and, after whistling loudly at their reported find, had gotten busy checking the Oklahoma laws about discovering a buried treasure on your own property. According to his research, if there was no indication it belonged to the government, a bank or business, or someone and their heirs, then it was "finders keepers." The only thing they had to contend with in the latter case would be giving the IRS their share, which would be about forty percent.

This morning Adam, Sage, and Evan returned to the cave, along with Ashley and Chris, to retrieve the rest of the treasure. It had taken them over two hours to bring it all to the surface and pack it onto the two flat trailers attached to Evan's and Chris's ATVs. Once they'd gotten it to the house, they'd broken open the two steel boxes and found them filled with gold coins.

Mr. Taft returned at Sage's insistence as they went through everything and found no indication of where the loot had come from nor who had stashed it in the cave. That meant it belonged to the Hammonds. From the information Adam and Chris had found online, Sage and her children were now millionaires—a fact she still couldn't fathom. Actually, they were multi-millionaires since the estimated value was ten million dollars, give or take a million, based on the number of silver bars and gold coins which they'd diligently counted.

Mr. Taft had contacted Lyle Dillinger at the bank and arranged for the treasure to be secured in the main vault until he could process the claim for Sage. He'd explained the silver could be sold through a dealer who specialized in gold and silver bullion, but the best choice for the gold coins was through an experienced auction house. He would find a reputable dealer and auction for her in the morning and arrange for all of it to be evaluated for sale.

"Sage." She turned to face Adam, who was standing with her lawyer and Lyle outside the vault's massive steel door. He was smiling at her. "Come on, it's after five o'clock. The clerks have all left, and Mr. Dillinger needs to close the bank. Unless you want us to lock you in there with it all night until you get used to the idea you're rich."

Shaking her head, she laughed as she exited the vault. "No. I'm good. Still in shock but good."

Lyle handed her several pieces of paper. "This is the paperwork and receipt for everything. Just let me know when to expect the assessors to come from whichever companies you choose to deal with."

"I'll call you with that information tomorrow, Lyle," Mr. Taft informed him.

Folding the papers into her purse, Sage glanced at the bank manager. "Thank you for staying open for us, Lyle. I guess it goes without saying my mortgage will be paid in full at some time in the very near future." She hadn't been able to resist pointing that out, even though she'd caught up with her payments as promised.

The man flushed and murmured a "thank you" before shutting the vault door and ensuring it was locked and sealed for the night. Adam took her hand, and they followed Mr. Taft to the front door, where the bank security guard was standing with two sheriff's deputies—another thing her lawyer had arranged to make sure they'd gotten to the bank safely.

When they stepped outside, Sage wasn't surprised to see a large, buzzing crowd of people waiting for them— word definitely spreads fast in a small town. A multitude of questions were thrown at her and Adam, along with many congratulations. It took them a good ten minutes to get back to her rented truck, which the security guard had moved away from the bank entrance for them after everything had been unloaded from the covered tail bed.

She *was* surprised to see Bart Sherman leaning against the side of her vehicle, but Adam seemed to have expected to run into him. He held out his hand to the older man. "How'd you know it was up there?"

Sherman grinned as he shook Adam's hand. Confused, Sage glanced back and forth between the two men. "What do you mean?"

"I suspect Bart knew the treasure was up there, and it's why he's been trying to purchase your land over the past few years."

The man didn't appear ashamed as he shrugged. "I'd found an old family diary in a wall at my house when we were renovating a few years back. In it, my great-great-great-granddaddy had been with his best friend—Mark's ancestor—when the man was shot during what was supposed to have been a friendly poker game. Edward Hammond survived the wound long enough for my name-sake to get him back to the Hammond's ranch. According to what my forefather wrote, Edward told him about a trea-sure he'd buried up on the hill and swore him to secrecy—apparently, Edward didn't trust banks. He asked him to make sure his widow and children were taken care of. The problem was Edward died before revealing the exact loca-tion. My forefather never found it, and I've searched my property and the state property beyond that with metal detectors over the years, with no success."

"And the only place you couldn't legally search was Sage's property," Adam concluded.

As Sage gaped at him, Bart shrugged his shoulders again, and his grin widened. "I may be a bastard some-times, but I still follow the law. Congratulations, Sage. Now I have to figure out what to do in my spare time. I think I'll start with selling that damn metal detector."

With a tip of his hat and a grin, he pushed off the truck and walked away.

———— ♥ ————

Four Months Later . . .

SHANE SLAPPED ADAM ON HIS SHOULDER AND THEN PULLED A BEER out of one of the many coolers on the back porch. "How's it feel to be a married man?"

"Give me a break. It's only been . . ." He glanced at his watch and grinned. ". . . thirty-six minutes since the reverend said, 'I now pronounce you man and wife.'"

They were standing on the back porch, watching the festivities around them. About a hundred people, kids included, were scattered around the backyard. Shane, his wife Nicole, and their three kids had flown in two days ago, while Sage's family had arrived earlier in the week. It looked like half the town had shown up for the nuptials and massive pig roast that followed.

Three weeks ago, Adam had surprised Sage with an engagement ring that Maddie and Ashley had helped him pick out. They'd been godsends because his head had started spinning at all the choices. Ultimately, they'd all agreed upon an emerald-cut diamond in a platinum setting. It wasn't something she could wear all the time on a horse ranch, but the matching wedding ring was.

After he'd gotten down on one knee and proposed up at the lake, Sage had obviously said yes, but then shocked the hell out of him when she told him she wanted to get married as soon as possible. She'd already lost a man she loved and didn't want to waste any time after being lucky enough to find another man to love.

It had been amazing how their friends and family had pulled together once more and organized the wedding in three weeks. The pig roast was being catered so everyone could enjoy themselves, but the rest had been done with a whirlwind of planning. Adam and Sage had been married under an arched trellis of roses, with Ashley and Maddie as bridesmaids and Shane and Evan as groomsmen. Jenna had been the flower girl, while Matthew and his grandfather had walked Sage down the aisle and given her away. And just like that, Adam was a husband and a father—two somethings he'd never expected to be—and had thanked God for every day. He'd come so close several times to losing everything he hadn't known he'd wanted.

Seth Chapman had pled guilty to the charges of arson, assault, kidnapping, and attempted murder but had hung himself in his cell less than a week into his prison sentence. Adam and Sage had made an anonymous donation through Reverend Stevens to help with his children's future education. They both believed the three siblings shouldn't have to suffer and pay for the sins of their father.

Sage, Adam, Jenna, and Matthew had become celebrities of sorts. There had been many news agencies—print, online, and on TV—who'd come calling for interviews about their treasure trove. Of course, that also meant the scam artists had started showing up, asking for the family to fund their inane projects. They'd had to hire a private security company until they became old news, and people stopped showing up at the ranch at all hours begging for money. Sage and Adam had no problem helping people in need, but most of the requests had been made from plain old greed.

Glancing around, Adam spotted his new wife. She was talking with Anna and Trent Boone, their neighbors to the east. The older couple had approached them a few weeks ago with a proposal. They had decided to sell their eighty-acre ranch and retire to Florida, where their daughter and family lived. With Sage's new windfall, the Boones had wanted to give her the first opportunity to purchase the land and had even named a reasonable price, being that they'd known her in-laws and then her for years. After talking it over, Adam and Sage agreed it would be perfect since they planned on expanding not only the horse breeding on the ranch but also that of the llamas and sheep. That meant they'd be hiring more ranch hands in addition to the two who had started last month.

"Here. This is for you." Shane handed Adam a thick, white envelope.

"What's this?"

His foster brother took a swig from his beer. "Open it, you twit."

Adam snorted and put down his beer so he could open the envelope. Sage and Nicole, who was carrying her daughter, Melanie, climbed the porch steps and walked toward the two men. Sage was beautiful in the simple, ivory lace sundress she'd picked out for the wedding, along with the ivory cowgirl boots. For his part, Adam had worn an ivory, western-style dress shirt with a bolero tie paired with black pants and boots.

Pulling the papers out of the envelope, Adam unfolded them as Sage sidled up and wrapped an arm around his waist. "What's this?"

"Adam's share of Harry and Barbara's estate," Shane replied as he took his daughter from his wife. "I figured it was time for him to take over his own accounts."

Dumbfounded, Adam's mouth dropped as he shuffled through the papers. "Um . . . what the heck? Shane . . .

there's a lot more zeroes here than there should be. There's no way Harry and Barbara left me this much money."

Sage gasped as she spied the total amount of the investment accounts' worth at the bottom of the page.

His brother grinned. "Oh, there was much less than that before my wife developed a nose for investing. There would've been more, but in the beginning, we took a gamble with our money before adding yours to the mix. Needless to say, you're now a very rich man and not because you married into it."

"Believe it or not," Nicole said, "it all started in my book club. One of the women brought her daughter, who is a stockbroker, in to talk to us about forming an investment group. She taught us how to research companies and analyze the market. We started off small, with everyone putting $100 into the kitty and investing it. Within two years, more than half of the women had retired from their jobs."

"Holy cow!" Sage was definitely impressed. "You'll have to tell me what to invest some of our money in."

"I'd be happy to. Not everything we've picked has paid off, and a few tanked horribly, but most of them have done really well."

Turning to her husband, Sage said, "I have a suggestion. Since we are no longer in desperate need of money, why don't you do something special with that? I mean, if you want."

"Like what?" He was still gaping at the paperwork.

"Like opening a youth center—kind of like a YMCA or something."

Shane bounced Melanie on his hip. "You could teach boxing and self-defense."

"You could teach anything the kids want to learn,"

Nicole added. "Stuff that's not really taught in school due to the curriculums, but kids should learn anyway."

A smile spread across Adam's face as he envisioned what they were all suggesting. "I think that's an awesome idea. How's this sound? The Harry and Barbara Brooks Youth Center."

"I think they'd be honored, bro. It's the perfect name." Shane actually looked a little teary-eyed as the two women agreed with the name.

Turning to Sage, Adam pulled her into his arms. "Will you volunteer to teach horse breeding? Because we both know home-ec is way out of your league."

She threw her head back and laughed. "Absolutely. We can do anything you want."

"Mommy! Adam!" Matthew came running toward them with Jenna on his heels. "Is it time?"

"Is it what time?" Adam asked as he made room for the two children to join the hug.

Jenna rolled her eyes in exasperation. "To tell us what the surprise is?"

"Surprise? Did we mention a surprise?" They had been teasing the kids for the past few days about a big surprise that wouldn't be revealed until after the wedding.

"AAAAdaaammm!"

The adults laughed at her tone as Adam squatted down to their level. "Oh, yeah. Your mom and I did mention a surprise. How would you like to go on our honeymoon with us? It just so happens we have two extra tickets to Disney World."

"Yay!" Both kids yelled and jumped up and down. "We're going to Disney World!"

As they ran off to tell their friends and cousins, Adam

stood and pulled his wife close again. "Have I told you how much I love you?"

She brushed her lips against his. "You tell me every time you look at me."

The other couple stepped away, giving them some alone time, but Adam didn't notice. For the first time in years, he felt as if his entire world was on its correct axis. Everything was just right. Somehow, someway, God had forgiven him and sent this beautiful woman to be his wife, along with two wonderful children. He didn't know what was down the road for all of them, but he would take each moment that would come and treasure it for the rest of his life.

———————— ♥ ————————

Ready for another great adventure?
Check out *Cold Feet: Largo Ridge Book 1*

THEY BOTH COME HOME TO LARGO RIDGE FOR DIFFERENT reasons...can they leave the past behind and risk their hearts again?

Regina calls off her wedding at the last minute—she couldn't marry someone she loved but wasn't in love with. Only one man fell into that category—Buck. However, after their one and only kiss years ago, he'd turned tail and run, leaving her confused and heartbroken.

The last thing Buck expects a few days after retiring from the military is to inherit a ski resort. That solves his problem of deciding what to do now that he's a civilian again. But he also has to face his PTSD and one big regret head-on.

For six years, his best friend's sister, Regina, had been out of sight but not quite out of Buck's mind. Now, with them both living in Largo Ridge again, it's getting harder to ignore the attraction growing stronger between them.

Does Buck have the courage to stand up and love the woman his heart knows is his? And will Regina let him?

Also by

Samantha Cole

***Denotes titles/series that are available on select digital sites only. Paperbacks and audiobooks are available on most book sites.

***The Trident Security Series

Leather & Lace

His Angel

Waiting For Him

Not Negotiable: A Novella

Topping The Alpha

Watching From the Shadows

Whiskey Tribute: A Novella

Tickle His Fancy

No Way in Hell: A Steel Corp/Trident Security Crossover (co-authored with J.B. Havens)

Absolving His Sins

Option Number Three: A Novella

Salvaging His Soul

Trident Security Field Manual

Torn In Half: A Novella

Don't Fight It

Don't Shoot the Messenger

THE MALONE BROTHERS SERIES

*Her Secret (*Formerly, *Take the Money and Run)*

*Her Sleuth (*Formerly *The Devil's Spare Change)*

LARGO RIDGE SERIES

Cold Feet

ANTELOPE ROCK SERIES

(CO-AUTHORED WITH J.B. HAVENS)

Wannabe in Wyoming

Wistful in Wyoming

AWARD-WINNING STANDALONE BOOKS

The Road to Solace

Scattered Moments in Time: A Collection of Short Stories & More

***THE BID ON LOVE SERIES

(WITH 7 OTHER AUTHORS!)

Going, Going, Gone: Book 2

***THE COLLECTIVE: SEASON TWO

(WITH 7 OTHER AUTHORS!)

Angst: Book 7

***SPECIAL COLLECTIONS

Trident Security Series: Volume I

About

USA Today Bestselling Author and Award-Winning Author Samantha Cole is a retired policewoman and former paramedic. Using her life experiences and training, she strives to find the perfect mix of suspense and romance for her readers to enjoy.

Awards:

Wannabe in Wyoming (co-authored by J.B. Havens) won the bronze medal in the 2021 Readers' Favorite Awards in the General Romance category.

Scattered Moments in Time, won the gold medal in the 2020 Readers' Favorite Awards in the Fiction Anthology category.

The Road to Solace (formerly *The Friar*), won the silver medal in the 2017 Readers' Favorite Awards in the Contemporary Romance category.

Samantha has over thirty-five books published throughout several different series as well as a few standalone novels. A full list can be found on her website.

Sexy Six-Pack's Sirens Group on Facebook
Website: www.samanthacoleauthor.com
Newsletter: www.smarturl.it/SSPNL

facebook.com/SamanthaColeAuthor

twitter.com/SamanthaCole222

instagram.com/samanthacoleauthor

amazon.com/Samantha-A-Cole/e/B00X53K3X8

bookbub.com/profile/samantha-a-cole

goodreads.com/SamanthaCole

pinterest.com/samanthacoleaut

Printed in Great Britain
by Amazon

24345430R00119